## "How long was it, that last time you and Jack were reunited?"

"Five weeks." Hope prayed it would shut Guy up.

"Five weeks? Long enough to conceive, have a pregnancy confirmed and get the divorce papers drawn up...."

"That's not the way it was! I never intended going back to Jack...."

Guy's lips formed a thin, cruel smile. "Maybe you should have stuck with me.... But then you couldn't be quite sure I could give you a baby, could you? Whereas my brother already had...."

*ALISON FRASER* was born and brought up in the far north of Scotland. She studied English literature at university and taught math for a while, then became a computer programmer. She took up writing as a hobby and it is still very much so, in that she doesn't take it too seriously! Currently Alison still lives in Scotland, with her two young children, two dogs, but only one husband!

### Books by Alison Fraser

HARLEQUIN PRESENTS
1425—TIME TO LET GO
1675—LOVE WITHOUT REASON
1753—TAINTED LOVE

# ALISON FRASER

## The Strength of Desire

# *Harlequin Books*

TORONTO • NEW YORK • LONDON
AMSTERDAM • PARIS • SYDNEY • HAMBURG
STOCKHOLM • ATHENS • TOKYO • MILAN
MADRID • WARSAW • BUDAPEST • AUCKLAND

ISBN 0-373-11836-8

THE STRENGTH OF DESIRE

First North American Publication 1996.

Copyright © 1995 by Alison Fraser.

# CHAPTER ONE

TEARS streamed down Hope's face as the radio played the song for which Jack was best known:

'The sun in your hair,
Pure gold.
The sky in your eyes,
Cloudless blue.
How can I not love you?
The stars in——

She switched it off, and sank down on a chair. It was a shock. Not the song, but the announcement beforehand: 'Jacques Delacroix died last night in a road accident.'

Why had no one told her? Why hadn't *Guy*? The thought of Jack's brother could still make her angry. Her mind quickly moved elsewhere.

Maxine. She needed to tell Maxine before anyone else did. How would she react? She was difficult at the best of times.

My fault, Hope acknowledged, all too aware of the way her daughter was going. At twelve she could pass for fourteen—a moody, resentful fourteen. My fault because I was too young.

Seventeen she had been when she'd met Jacques—or Jack, as he'd been called. Just turned eighteen when she'd married him. Pregnant shortly after. Ridiculous.

That's what Guy had said, of course. Guy Delacroix—Jack's little brother. Hope's lips twisted at the term. That was what Jack had called him and that was what Hope had expected. A younger, paler version of Jack. But Guy had been in no one's shadow.

5

She remembered their first meeting. It had been at a London restaurant. Jack had invited him to lunch to meet Jack's future bride. He'd driven up from Cornwall where he lived and had arrived late. Jack and she had already been seated at the rear of the restaurant and had not noticed his approach.

He had appeared at their table and Hope had just stared in surprise. Jack's little brother had turned out to be anything but little.

At six feet two, he was several inches taller and broader than Jack, and, on first glance, actually looked older, with his dark hair and steel-grey eyes and a slightly weathered complexion.

The brothers were totally unalike. At thirty-five Jack could have passed for twenty-five. Blond, boyish and handsome, he was a slim five feet ten. He had all the charm of an older man with the outlook of a much younger one. The age-gap between Hope and Jack— seventeen years—seemed nothing.

Nothing until Guy Delacroix pointed it out. He stared at her, long and hard, then spoke to Jacques, excluding her.

He said, '*Es-tu fou, Jacques? Elle est une enfant.*'

He did not look at Hope. If he had, he might have seen from her face that she wasn't stupid. She could certainly translate basic French: 'Are you mad, Jack? She is a child.'

She waited for Jacques to deny, to resent, to explode, but he just laughed. '*Peut-être. Mais une très belle enfant, n'est-ce pas?*' He smiled at his brother.

Hope could translate that, too. O level French was one of the few she'd managed to acquire at the trendy boarding-school where her father had sent her.

'Perhaps,' Jack conceded. 'But a very beautiful child, isn't she?'

Guy's eyes slid back to her. From the expression on his face, he didn't agree.

Hope didn't care what he thought of her looks. She responded, '*Je ne suis pas une enfante ni stupide.*'

'I am not a child or stupid,' she informed Guy Delacroix, blue eyes narrowing in temper.

Jack looked surprised, then laughed again. He had not known she could speak French, but was unembarrassed by it.

If anything, his brother looked even further down his long French nose, his thin lips twisting. Hope's first impression of a powerfully handsome man was rapidly forgotten, as she thought him mean-eyed and cold.

'Do you wish me to apologise?' he directed at her, not one degree warmer.

'Not if it's going to kill you,' she retorted in a careless tone.

They exchanged looks again, registering their true feelings. Hate at first sight.

Jack seemed amused as he suggested, 'Shall we start again? In English, this time, I think... Hope Gardener, meet Guy Delacroix. My fiancée. My brother.' He nodded from one to the other.

After a moment's hesitation, Guy Delacroix muttered a scrupulously polite, 'Pleased to meet you,' as he extended his hand towards her.

His personality seemed to change with his language. From Gallic temper to English dispassion in one easy move. At any rate, it was the first and last time he ever spoke French in front of her.

Hope wondered which was real as she reluctantly returned his brief handshake and he sat down. She recalled what Jack had told her about the Delacroix family. Their mother was English, from Cornwall. She had married a Frenchman and they had spent their early years in Paris. When their father, Armand Delacroix, had died, Jack had been twelve, Guy seven. A couple of years later they had returned to live in Cornwall.

On first impression, Guy had seemed the more French, but, as she listened to his ensuing conversation with Jack, she revised that opinion. He was a lawyer who talked in dry, lawyer terms. Jack allowed him to handle his business affairs. With Guy based in Cornwall, inconveniently far from London, Hope assumed Jack did this as a favour.

Not that Guy Delacroix appeared particularly grateful. If anything, his tone to Jack was one of reproof as they talked of contracts and percentages. Jack, in contrast, was his usual affable self, uninterested in money or the business matters behind his work as a performer.

Hope was on his side. Jack was an artist. He sang in a gravelly voice that was adored by millions of women, and wrote love-songs that wrenched the heart. Who could blame him if he didn't want to discuss the boring mechanics behind the brilliant concert performances he gave?

'Come on, Guy,' he eventually said to his brother, 'lighten up. Hope doesn't want to listen to the niceties of contractual law. Do you, *chérie*?' He smiled sexily at her, and she smiled back, the look in her eyes sharing secrets.

'She might, if it stops you ending up bankrupt,' Guy Delacroix's voice intruded gratingly.

Hope's eyes switched to him, questioning. What was he implying? That she was just interested in Jack's wealth?

That was the way Jack took it, laughing a little as he said, 'My little brother is a cynic. He thinks you just love me for my money... Why don't we convince him otherwise?' he suggested silkily, and leaned across the table to kiss her.

Hope wasn't really given a chance to respond. She gasped a little in surprise and Jack slid his tongue into her mouth with an intimacy that quite shocked her. Before she could sort out her feelings, he broke off the kiss and grinned at his brother.

Hope's face suffused with colour. Because they were in a booth at the rear of the restaurant, only Guy

Delacroix had witnessed the kiss, but that was enough. Though his face was rigid, there was disgust in his eyes.

Jack seemed unaware of it as he laughed, 'I'm a lucky man,' then started relaying plans for their wedding.

He explained that Hope didn't want a big ceremony, and they had decided on a register office. Jack asked Guy to be a witness. Hope knew instantly that Guy would refuse, even before he went through the motions of asking the date and discovering he had court commitments he couldn't break.

Jack was clearly disappointed. He had no suspicion that his brother might be lying. Hope caught Guy Delacroix's eye again, and was certain of it. He had no intention of giving support to a marriage he considered disastrous from the outset.

No, Guy wasn't a hypocrite. He never pretended to be anything but displeased. When Jack excused himself during the meal, his brother didn't hang about. He went on the attack within seconds.

'How old are you? Sixteen?' he guessed, lips thinning.

'Nearly eighteen,' Hope snapped back, immediately on the defensive.

'*That* old,' he muttered, drily sarcastic. 'I assume you've asked for the day off school—for the wedding, I mean,' he added in the same vein.

'I left school last year,' Hope relayed, quite unnecessarily, she was sure.

A black brow was raised in disapproval. 'At sixteen.'

'Yes. Right.' Hope gave up trying to win her future brother-in-law's approval. Temper made her run on, 'Uneducated as well as young and stupid. Why don't I just give you a list of all my faults, then you won't have to bother grubbing around for them yourself?'

He looked taken aback for a moment, having underestimated her ability to fight back, but it didn't discourage him.

'Why don't you?' he echoed, bland in the face of her temper.

'Let's see,' Hope muttered tightly. 'Well, I have no job or prospects of one. I have no money and, very soon, no home. I get hay fever in the summer, and chest complaints in the winter... Oh, and the women in my family tend to develop thick ankles by thirty,' she added, the most ridiculous thing she could think of saying.

Just for a moment she glimpsed the merest hint of amusement on his mouth, but it quickly disappeared. Guy Delacroix had decided to disapprove of her on sight, and nothing was going to change his opinion.

'Your family...' He picked out another line of attack. 'How do they feel about your marrying someone seventeen years older?'

'They feel nothing,' she retorted, and told him bluntly, 'My mother died when I was born, my father a couple of months ago.'

His eyes narrowed, as if he acknowledged the pain of the last, but he expressed no sympathy. Instead he asked, 'Did you meet Jack before or after he died?'

'I've known Jack for years,' she could claim quite truthfully. 'My father produced a couple of his early albums.'

'Gardener...' He mused over her name, then worked out, 'Max Gardener was your father?'

She nodded, surprised that Jack hadn't told him that.

He read her mind, saying, 'Jack doesn't believe in giving much detail. I heard you were young, blonde and beautiful... and, of course, the love of his life. That was all.'

But he hadn't believed it, Hope realised from Guy's tone. He thought she was just another of Jack's conquests.

'Have you slept with him yet?' he added, almost offhandedly.

'What?' Hope stared at him incredulously.

'Have you slept with him?' he repeated, as if it were a quite normal question to ask a complete stranger.

'I... We... It's none of your business!' she finally exploded.

He watched as colour suffused her face. 'You haven't,' he concluded. 'Well, perhaps you should. I can recommend it as one of the quickest ways of discovering incompatibility.'

'How do you know we're incompatible?' Hope retorted angrily.

'Apart from the seventeen-year age-gap, you mean?' His tone was heavily ironic.

'You're just jealous!' she accused in return.

He smiled thinly. 'Don't flatter yourself. You might be beautiful, but schoolgirls aren't my thing.'

Hope glared, sure he'd deliberately misunderstood. 'Jealous of Jack, I meant. His talent. His fame. His____'

'Money?' he suggested wryly.

Hope went from glaring to fuming. Guy Delacroix obviously had her written off as a gold-digger and wasn't about to change his mind.

He continued at her furious silence, 'No, I can't say I've ever been jealous of Jack. I have sufficient money for my own needs. Talent... Well, admittedly writing love-songs is hardly my forte.' He made a slight face, dismissing such a skill as unimportant. 'And fame, well, that's a dubious privilege at the best of times... But I suppose it all seems very glamorous to you.'

'I'm not that naïve.' Hope was well aware of the price of fame. Her father had once been famous as a record producer—and rich. But he'd paid for it. When the popularity of his music had waned he'd felt a failure, and sought solace in a whisky bottle.

'No, I suppose not,' Guy Delacroix conceded. 'You must have met many famous people through your father.'

'When I was little,' Hope replied, 'but not lately... People in show business don't like to associate with failures. They think it's catching,' she commented cynically.

He raised a brow, surprised by her astuteness. 'What did he die from?' he asked bluntly.

'Cancer—not catching either,' she said on a bitter note, 'but it still kept them away... Apart from his funeral—they returned in droves for that. It's a pity he missed it. He would have appreciated seeing his ex-wives sobbing their little hearts out at the loss of their alimony.'

'How many?' he enquired.

'Ex-wives? Three, but only two attended the funeral,' Hope recounted.

He pulled a wry face at the number. 'Does that total include your mother?'

'No, she was never an ex,' Hope declared stiffly, but didn't expand on it.

She knew, for her father had told her often enough, that her mother had been the great love in his life. It had sounded sentimental, but it had also been true. It was a fact that each wife, in turn, had come to face.

'Is that where you met Jack again? At the funeral?'

'No, he came before, in the last week or two when Dad became really ill. Then later he offered to help with the arrangements.' Hope's voice revealed how grateful she'd been to Jack. He'd been a true friend to them both, and her love for him had developed even as she'd struggled with the pain of grief.

'That was good of him.' Guy's tone was flat, but there was a look of scepticism in his eye.

'What's that supposed to mean?' Hope demanded in return.

'Nothing, just...' He hesitated for the first time, then switched to saying, 'Look, we got off on the wrong foot. My fault, I admit. I misunderstood the situation.'

'That's all right.' Hope was ready to forgive him. She didn't want to be enemies with Jack's family.

'However,' he continued in a serious vein, 'I still feel you really should consider what you're doing. You're only seventeen. You've just lost your father. You're vulnerable...'

'I can take care of myself,' Hope claimed, but not quite convincingly, as her fingers plucked agitatedly at the tablecloth.

'Fine, take care of yourself,' he echoed, stilling her hand with his. 'Just don't let Jack do it for you.'

He spoke with such force that Hope's eyes flew to his. She met their steady grey gaze and for a moment saw the man behind the dispassionate mask. She sensed his strength, and was scared by his certainty. For a moment she almost listened to him, then Jack suddenly returned to the table.

'Holding hands?' Jack enquired, not quite casually, as he tried to assess the situation.

Hope flushed although she had nothing to feel guilty about. Not then. She hastily pulled her fingers from Guy's grip.

He was unflustered, drawling to his brother, 'Not exactly. I was just trying to persuade Hope that she was about to make the biggest mistake of her young life.'

'By marrying me?' Jack concluded, and laughed out loud when his brother nodded. 'That's what I love about my little brother. You can always trust him to be totally up front about things... Well, you're wrong this time, Guy. Hope and I are going to make the distance. Just watch...'

'Just watch.' Hope shut her eyes as she recalled Jack's words all those years ago. Guy had watched all right. He'd watched his words come true. He'd watched their marriage disintegrate. He'd...more than watched.

Hope caught the direction of her thoughts and put a brake on them. She wasn't going down that road again.

She looked at her watch, and, realising she'd lost almost an hour, got up quickly to fix her face.

She'd just finished washing when Maxine announced her presence with the usual banging doors. She hadn't time to put on make-up before her daughter tracked her down to the bathroom. For once Hope wished she'd taken a less liberal attitude on privacy.

Maxine walked in, took one look at her face and demanded, 'What's wrong? You've been crying.'

It sounded like an accusation, but then everything did at the moment with Maxine.

'No... Well, actually, yes.' Hope wished she'd rehearsed this speech. 'It's...it's your father.'

'My father? Don't tell me—he's dead,' Maxine said, but purely for dramatic effect.

While Hope searched futilely for the right words, her face gave away the truth.

Maxine shook her head as if denying it, then started to back away from her.

'I'm sorry, darling.' Hope made to reach out a hand but her daughter kept backing away. 'A car accident. I don't know the details. It was on the radio. I'm sorry——'

'Well, I'm not!' Maxine almost shouted at her. 'And don't expect me to cry! Just don't...'

With that, Maxine turned and ran from the room.

Hope followed her daughter to her room. She found her face down on the bed, crying like a baby.

Hope sat down beside her and put a comforting hand on her shoulder.

Maxine stiffened, then, turning on her back, sobbed out, 'I don't care. I hate him! I hate him!'

'I know. I know. It's all right,' Hope said in comforting tones, and stroked strands of hair from her daughter's tear-soaked face.

Maxine looked at her in utter misery, then accused, 'It was your fault, all your fault!'

It hurt. Of course it hurt, but Hope did not retaliate. Maxine was right. The whole mess was her fault.

Hope contained her own feelings, but Maxine read the pain in her mother's eyes, and hesitated between attack and remorse. In the end she sat up and threw her arms round Hope's neck, and began crying again.

'I didn't mean it! I didn't mean it!' she cried into her mother's neck.

'No, I know.' Hope held her daughter and rocked her gently, as she had when Maxine was a baby.

But her thoughts were elsewhere. With another baby. A baby held briefly in her arms, all those years ago.

She remembered how much she'd wanted children, how she'd imagined being a mother would make her complete. She hadn't questioned why she'd felt incomplete.

She'd also imagined Jack would be happy, too, but, of course, she'd been quite wrong...

'You're what?' he had almost shouted at her when she'd told him.

The joy had drained from her face as she'd repeated, 'I'm pregnant. Three months.'

She'd waited and waited. For a smile. A flicker of happiness. A gesture of concern. Anything other than Jack's expression of utter dismay.

He'd recovered himself eventually, saying, 'It's a shock. I thought we'd have some time together. We agreed...'

'I know.' Hope nodded. They had agreed to take precautions, but something had gone wrong. 'I didn't plan it. I didn't realise you'd mind so much.'

'It's not that,' Jack denied, although his lack of enthusiasm was almost palpable. He strode across to the drinks cabinet and fixed himself a stiff drink, before running on, 'It just doesn't fit in very well with our plans. My world tour starts in three months and won't finish before the baby would be born... Perhaps we should wait.'

'Wait?' Hope echoed, confused. 'Wait before you go on tour, you mean?'

'No, that's impossible. The tour can't be cancelled,' he told her firmly. 'I just thought... Well, if you're only three months along...' He left the idea hanging there.

Hope caught it and her heart sank. 'You think we should cancel the baby.' She finally said the words aloud. They were like stones in her heart.

'I'd hardly term it that,' Jack said, 'but, yes, I feel we should consider the alternatives...'

Perhaps Maxine was right. It really was her fault. If she'd listened to Jack, terminated that baby and waited for another, their marriage might have survived. But that baby had been real to her, a person even in the early stages of pregnancy. To terminate on a matter of convenience had been abhorrent to her.

'Look, Maxine.' She spoke quietly to her daughter now. 'I realise you haven't seen much of your father over the years, but, as I've explained before, it was never personal to you.'

'I know—he didn't like children.' Maxine grossly simplified what Hope had actually told her over the years. 'Then why did he come those times? Why did he bother?'

Hope had asked herself the same question many times. After ten years' silence, Jack had turned up on impulse on her doorstep one afternoon, and been all charm to a daughter who, at ten, was already promising to be beautiful. With Hope's blue eyes and wide, smiling mouth, Maxine still managed to look quite different, her features more defined and her hair a mass of thick black waves.

'It would have been better if he'd never come,' Maxine said now, her tears turned to anger as she scrambled off the bed and went to wash in the basin in her room.

Hope agreed with her, but at the time she'd been unable to control the situation. Jack had wanted a daughter, for a while at least, and Maxine had wanted a father. But Jack's interest hadn't, of course, lasted.

'I'm sorry about the way things turned out, Maxine,' Hope said gently, when her daughter finished drying her face.

She realised the inadequacy of her words even before Maxine looked at her with accusing eyes. 'Are you? You never wanted me to go places with him.'

Hope remained silent. It was true enough. In fact, after a year of Jack letting Maxine down with a string of broken promises, Hope had deliberately put an end to the relationship.

'That's Katie,' Maxine added as the doorbell downstairs rang. 'We're going to do our homework together. I'd better let her in.'

'Yes, OK.' Hope blinked a little as her daughter disappeared downstairs to greet her best friend. She heard them laughing in the hallway. From utter misery to girlish giggles in one short move.

How wonderful it would be to be twelve again. To forget so easily. To live in the present. To be free of the past.

Hope had never quite managed it. She was thirty-two next birthday, and had spent twelve years on her own, yet she was still haunted by the past, still tortured by a sense of failure...

She was six months pregnant and miserable. She had read that women bloomed in similar circumstances but she seemed to have wilted. Jack was fed up with her. She didn't blame him. She was fed up with herself.

'There's no choice,' Jack said for the hundredth time as they drove down to Cornwall. 'It would have been different if your pregnancy was straightforward, but, with your iron-levels, you'd be fainting all over the place. You can't come on tour with me and you can't stay at home.'

'I could have stayed with Vicki,' Hope lamented, still hoping that Jack might change his mind.

'Vicki,' Jack repeated her best friend's name, 'is a nice kid, but, be honest, how much use would she be in a crisis? She is the original dizzy blonde.'

Hope bristled silently, but couldn't deny the truth of it. Vicki had been enormous fun at boarding-school and a good friend since. Catering for the needs of a pregnant woman, however, wasn't one of her talents.

'Anyway, Vicki's asked if she can come on the tour,' Jack reminded her. 'I don't know if she'll be much help, but, as a favour to you, I've agreed.'

'All right,' Hope sighed, resigned to her fate.

Three months staying in the wilds of Cornwall with Jack's mother. That she didn't mind. It was the fact that the lady also happened to be brother Guy's mother. Did this mean she might have regular contact with him?

She had not seen Guy Delacroix since their first meeting. He had been as good as his word and not attended their wedding, although his mother had.

In her late fifties, Caroline Delacroix had seemed younger. Her hair was silvery-blonde and her face, despite signs of aging, still had an English-rose bloom to it. She was a sharp, intelligent woman, without being an intellectual, and she spoke her mind.

'I don't suppose you're going to listen to me, but I think you're probably too young and certainly too good for my son,' she'd finally announced, after they'd taken tea together.

Already liking the woman, Hope hadn't been too upset by her comments. 'Your other son's already said the same. Well, the too young part, anyway.'

'Yes, I understand Guy tried to warn you,' Caroline had confirmed, 'and that you and he didn't exactly hit it off.'

'Not so you'd notice.' Hope had made a slight face. 'What did he say?'

'Nothing much. Just that you were "bloody impossible",' his mother had confided, but with an amused air that softened any offence. 'With Guy, that could be a compliment. He doesn't like women who fall over themselves to please him. Unfortunately, most do.'

'Well, this one won't,' Hope had vowed then to Caroline Delacroix, and vowed now, as she travelled down to the Delacroix family home in Cornwall.

It was actually her first visit. Jack's mother had come to London to meet her before the wedding, and, almost straight after it, had disappeared on a two-month tour of China. On her return, she'd stopped over briefly in London, issuing an invitation for Hope to come down to Cornwall any time she liked. But Jack's work schedule had precluded even a weekend trip, and Hope's only recent contact with her mother-in-law had been over the telephone. The older woman had been pleased at the prospect of being a grandmother, and had willingly agreed to her spending the final months of her pregnancy in Cornwall, but Hope still felt she was intruding when they finally drove up to the Delacroix family home.

It was called Heron's View, and Hope could immediately see why. It sat on a clifftop overlooking the Atlantic and was the most wonderful house she had ever seen. It was a house from a fairy-story, with turrets and towers, walled gardens and secret places. It was large and imposing without being grandiose or ostentatious. It suggested a bygone era, of the years before the First World War, when large families were the norm, and Hope could imagine voices of children echoing through the twists and turns of the many stone passages.

'It belonged to my father's family. There were seven of them, and he inherited as the eldest,' Caroline relayed as they stood in the hall which was at the centre of the house, with rooms leading off and a wide staircase leading up. 'He, in turn, gave it to my eldest sister who never married. She died a couple of years ago.'

'Is that when you moved in?' Hope quizzed.

'Oh, no, I've always lived here——' Caroline smiled round the shabby hall with pleasure '—apart from the ten years I spent in France. I returned with the boys here. My father gave it to Hetty because he felt I was secure financially, but it was always a family house. Hetty helped me bring the boys up, too, although she was rather more interested in her dogs.'

'She had six,' Jack put in. 'Red setters. She dedicated her life to breeding a Cruft's champion.'

'Did she manage?' Hope asked, interested.

'Not exactly,' Caroline replied, 'but one of her dogs was the grandfather of a supreme champion... Anyway, I hope you like dogs.'

Hope nodded. 'We had a retriever when I was little.'

'Good,' Caroline nodded, 'because Guy seems to have inherited some of Hetty's fanaticism. He keeps three setters, and each is as mad as the other. I insisted he lock them away until you were settled.'

'Guy keeps his dogs here.' Hope trusted that was all she meant.

But a deep, drawling voice answered her. 'Guy keeps himself here, too,' and, as Hope's eyes were drawn, horrified, to the back of the hall, Guy Delacroix emerged from the shadows.

'There you are,' Caroline greeted her son with fond exasperation. 'I called to you that they'd arrived but you seemed to have disappeared.'

'I was locking up the hounds, as requested,' he answered his mother, but his eyes slid to Hope, acknowledging the difference in her.

When they had first met, she had been as slim as a reed and in the best of health, her long blonde hair silky, her complexion soft and clear. In a maternity dress, with hair escaping from a hastily tied ribbon and her skin with a bluey-white tinge, she looked like the drudge she felt.

'You've changed,' he said bluntly, and Hope could have cried.

But she was tougher than that. She asked herself if she cared what he thought, and, lying to herself, decided she didn't.

'You haven't,' she answered him, and her tone said it was a pity.

Jack recognised the enmity between them, and, if anything, was amused. But a frown lined Caroline's forehead, as it occurred to her that life at Heron's View might be less than smooth in the coming months.

Guy was unruffled, continuing, 'I assume no one informed you I was in residence.'

Before Hope could answer, Jack slipped in, 'I didn't want to scare her off, little brother.'

'No, I don't imagine you did,' Guy echoed drily, and clearly meant more than his words said.

Jack appeared to understand. He gave his brother a conspiratorial smile. It was not returned by Guy, however. He was stony-faced.

Hope wondered how these two men could be brothers. Jack was charm itself; Guy was charmless.

Their mother decided it was time to move things on. 'Would you like to see your room? Guy suggested you might prefer some privacy, so we've rearranged things to give you most of the west wing.'

'Thank you,' Hope acknowledged in a small voice, but didn't look at Guy. She wasn't fooled. It was the family that was to have privacy from her.

Caroline led the way upstairs while Guy and Jack went to take in her cases. The west wing, as the name suggested, was almost a separate part of the house. It was reached by a long corridor off the main stairway. As well as a large double bedroom, it boasted an adjoining bathroom and dressing-room. The most interesting feature, however, was a perfectly circular room inset in one of the turrets. It had been turned into a small sitting-room, with a wonderful view over the cliffs and the Atlantic beyond. From it led a staircase that wound down to the back courtyard.

Hope loved the room, and didn't hide her enthusiasm from Caroline. The older woman smiled in relief, saying, 'Oh, I am glad you like it. I thought Guy's taste might be a little functional for a young girl.'

'These are Guy's rooms?' Hope repeated, her face falling.

Caroline realised her mistake and quickly reassured her. 'Yes, but don't worry. You're not putting him out. He's only really here at the weekends, and he was quite happy to move to the east wing.'

Anywhere, as long as it was away from her, Hope thought for a moment, then told herself not to be so paranoid. Guy Delacroix mightn't be keen on her, but she wasn't that important to him.

And so it appeared, in the next couple of months as she lived in limbo in the house on the cliff. Caroline was kind without being effusive. Guy was largely absent. His work was based in Truro and during the week he stayed there. If she saw him at weekends, it was only in passing or at dinner on Sundays. Pleading sickness, she could miss even that contact. If things had not gone so drastically wrong with her pregnancy, they probably could have maintained their distance for her whole stay at Heron's View.

But things did go wrong. It was six weeks before the birth. She had seen almost as little of Jack as she had of his brother, with him returning only for the odd visit between concert dates. And separation had not improved their relationship. While she was tired from heavy pregnancy, he was running in overdrive from his tour. He longed to be doing, drinking, partying, carrying on as before, only he was chained to her by duty.

'It'll be all right after the baby,' he kept saying, and Hope felt the reassurance was as much for himself as for her.

It actually made her heart sink as she realised the life Jack was planning for them. The tours and the concerts and the travelling would continue. She would go with him. The baby would stay at home with a nanny.

But Hope couldn't share the vision. No matter how sick or how lonely she felt, she already loved the child inside her. To leave him, or her, would be an agony. But, if she didn't, she knew she might lose Jack.

She sometimes wondered if she'd lost him already. His visits were so infrequent. Only tears had extracted a promise from him to be at her side for the week before and after the birth.

In the end he didn't make it. The baby came early. It was terrifying.

She was alone. Caroline had offered to stay in, but Hope had insisted she go to her regular Friday bridge evening. Guy hadn't returned from Truro.

The storm began at nine. Normally Hope wasn't scared of a little lightning or thunder. But this wasn't a little; this was an electric display of pyrotechnics that lit up the sky. She watched at the window of her sitting-room as the waves crashed against the cliff-face and the rain came down in a sheet. She went to another window, looking on to the courtyard, and was in time to see a bolt of lightning flash out of the sky and seem to hit the roof of Heron's View. She started in surprise.

It was a couple of minutes before she realised it wasn't just her heart that was contracting with fright. The baby was coming. She tried not to panic. She had rehearsed in her mind so many times what they would do, but it had always been 'they'. Now she was on her own.

The thought occurred to her that she would always be on her own. It was a bleak prospect. She pushed it away and concentrated on the practicalities.

She went to the telephone to do the obvious—call an ambulance. The line was dead. She couldn't believe it. She banged down the receiver, as if that might cure some temporary fault. It didn't.

Once more she told herself not to panic, but it was harder now. What to do? Drive. Drive what? The old MGB Guy kept in one of the garages. Did it work? Where were the keys? Could she get her bump behind the steering-wheel?

A sob escaped her, but she stifled a second one. If she wanted this baby to live, she had to keep her head. Driving to the hospital wasn't feasible. She had to wait until Caroline arrived home; that could only be two hours away, maybe three. Meanwhile she had to go downstairs while she could still move. If she didn't, it was possible that Caroline might go to bed without checking on her.

She got to her feet and went out into the corridor and along to the main staircase. She held on tightly to the rail as she descended. She hadn't become too large in late pregnancy, but she'd remained tired and weak through low iron-levels. She was almost downstairs when another contraction ripped through her body. Clutching her swollen stomach, she sat down on the third step and tried to breathe the pain away.

It seemed an interminable time that she sat on that step, praying for help to come. The contractions were coming every five minutes when she heard the outer door bang open. She could have cried with relief.

With what seemed the last breath in her body, she called out, 'Caroline,' then gasped once more as another contraction tore through her. She threw her head back, her brow damp with the sweat of effort and fear.

But it wasn't Caroline.

Guy Delacroix came into the hall, rain dripping off his black hair. 'It's me.'

He took one look at Hope and assessed the situation.

She looked back—in horror. It should have been relief. Help was at last at hand. But her very first reaction was horror.

'You're in labour.' He frowned in disbelief.

She nodded.

'Have you called an ambulance?' he added.

'I tried,' she breathed out. 'The line seems to be dead.'

'I'll try again.' He crossed to the telephone in the hall.

She watched him as he confirmed that the line was dead. He seemed amazingly controlled, but then he wasn't the one in labour.

He looked at her again, judging the urgency of the situation, before saying, 'Right. I'll get my car back out of the garage and bring it round.'

He left her, and Hope struggled to contain her panic. She was scared for herself. She was scared for the baby. It was far too early.

Guy returned shortly. He must have run to the garage. When he appeared at the door, Hope tried to lift herself up, but the next contraction hit her just then. The wave of pain made her sink back on the step.

He walked over to her and waited until the pain subsided before helping her up.

'Put your arm round my shoulders,' he instructed quietly, and, bearing much of her weight, took her out to his car. He installed her in the back where she could stretch out.

'I'll write a note for my mother. Hopefully she'll follow on to be with you,' he informed her, and returned to the house.

He was gone only a minute or two, but it seemed like an age. He arranged over her a blanket he'd brought, before climbing into the front and setting the car in motion. Hope curled up like the foetus inside her and wished it were all over.

He didn't bother her with unnecessary conversation. He just drove. When she gasped with pain, he asked, 'How frequent are the contractions?'

'Every four or five minutes,' she answered, wondering if it would mean anything to him.

Perhaps it did, as he seemed to increase his speed. It was a tortuous route down the hillside from Heron's View to the main road, but he took the bends with practised ease, seemingly unaffected by the flashes of lightning that lit up the sky.

Hope was frightened, but his calmness helped her contain her own fear. They arrived at the hospital without mishap, and, after taking directions from a car-park attendant, Guy drove straight up to the maternity department entrance. Then he left her briefly to find a nurse, who recognised the situation as a far from normal labour and the next thing Hope knew she was on a hospital trolley being pushed along corridors to the delivery suite.

She was still dressed in her night gown and robe, and a midwife helped her out of the robe, but she indicated that she wished to keep her nightie on, especially with Guy Delacroix still at her side.

He stood frowning down at her, perhaps wondering how to extricate himself, then another contraction made her draw her knees up.

'Hold her hand, Dad,' the nurse instructed briskly. 'I think your baby's well on its way.'

He remained still for a moment. Hope waited for him to deny the identity that had been thrust upon him. Instead he took her hand in his.

'He's not——' Hope tried to explain the true situation, but another contraction ripped through her. It was the worst yet. She couldn't believe the pain.

She gripped Guy's hand as if she could transfer some of the pain to him. It seemed to help. At any rate, she had no breath left for explanations as the doctor on call appeared.

Everything happened very quickly after that. She had started to haemorrhage. The doctor decided a Caesarean was the only option. Before they could wheel her into an operating theatre, she lost consciousness, still holding Guy's hand.

They did their best, but it was already too late. Her baby, her first-born, had been a boy. A perfectly formed baby boy who had never drawn breath in the world outside.

Some time later she woke to find herself attached to a drip. Guy was by her side, waiting. He said no words. She saw the truth in his eyes.

She'd always considered him a cold, emotionless man, and perhaps he was, but that night he held her in his arms while she cried out her grief and bitterness at losing her first baby.

He was still there in the morning. He had sat by her bedside while she slept. He took her hand when she woke.

Hope bit back tears and said, 'I'm sorry,' for it should have been Jack who was there, Jack who was sharing her suffering.

He shook his head, and asked simply, 'How do you feel?'

'Empty.' Hope put a hand to her stomach to protect her baby. But he was gone. He was dead. 'Can I see him?'

'If that's what you want.' Guy accepted her need to see the baby as if it was the most natural thing in the world. 'I'll speak to the nurse.'

He arranged it for her. The baby was brought to her, wrapped in a blue shawl. Guy sat with her while she held her child for the first time, and the last. He let her cry over that small, lifeless human being, then held her again when she cried as they took the baby away.

Somehow she survived that terrible day, and what Guy had been to her remained their secret.

Caroline appeared in the afternoon. Because of the storm, she'd stayed overnight with a friend and had just returned to find Guy's note.

She took over from Guy at Hope's bedside, while he went to follow up the calls he'd already made to Jack, currently on the other side of the Atlantic.

Flowers with sympathy notes arrived before Jack finally did, a day later. Only then did Guy fade into the background, possibly relieved that his brother was there to grieve with her.

But, of course, he didn't. He talked, but his words weren't the right ones. He tried to console her with the idea that she had been too young for a baby. Only her body didn't think so. It longed to hold the life it had briefly created.

Jack had no desire to see their baby, either. It had never been real to him. Hope had given him a name—Samuel—but Jack never used it.

She remained in hospital for a week, then returned home to Heron's View. Jack went back to his tour, suggesting she join him when she was properly recovered.

Perhaps it was then that she should have left him, when her love for him had already died a little with their baby. But she just couldn't accept the failure. Growing up, she'd watched each of her father's marriages disintegrate with frightening ease. She'd promised herself that things would be different for her. She felt there was no choice but to stay with Jack.

It must have seemed weakness to Guy Delacroix. He continued to be kind to her after she left hospital, but the kindness changed to incredulity when she announced her intention over dinner one night of flying over to the States to be with Jack.

If Caroline Delacroix had any reservations, she kept them to herself. Guy waited until his mother left the room before he expressed his.

'You can't go,' he told her from across the table. 'You look like hell.'

'Thanks.' Hope pulled a face but took no offence. She was growing used to Guy's bluntness, and she was still grateful to him for looking after her during her labour, and afterwards.

'You know what I mean,' he accused gruffly. 'It's only been four weeks. The doctor said you needed to rest.'

'Well, I won't be working in America,' she countered.

'That isn't the point!' he went on in exasperation. 'Who's going to look after you if you do get sick? And don't say Jack. He can barely look after himself.'

Out of loyalty, Hope felt she should challenge the latter comment. The trouble was that she suspected it was true. Jack could not be relied on.

'I have to go,' she said simply. 'Jack's my husband.'

She considered it an adequate reason but Guy didn't, snapping back, 'That's a mistake you can remedy.'

This time Hope was hurt. 'Why are you so against me, Guy?'

'God, I'm not against you, Hope. That's the last thing I am. If you knew——' He stopped himself in mid-sentence, and changed to saying, 'I'm just worried about you. You're still so...'

'Young,' Hope concluded for him, and shook her head. 'No, I'm not, Guy. Not any more.'

Hope didn't think she'd ever be young again. Grief had made her old.

Guy understood, and his anger gave way to compassion. He reached across the table to lay his hand over hers. The gesture was too much for Hope. She didn't want his pity. She didn't want even to think what she might have wanted from Guy, had things been different.

She took her hand away and rushed from the dining-room. He didn't follow.

She left for the States just a day later, without talking to Guy again.

But she was to return.

# CHAPTER TWO

'THERE'S a man hanging around outside,' Maxine announced some time later, having tracked her mother down to the kitchen.

'A man?' Hope's mind returned sharply to the present.

'He's been there a couple of minutes,' Maxine relayed. 'I think he's deciding if he has the right address. He has it written down, but, of course, our nine has come loose and turned into a six... I'm sure I told you.'

'Yes.' Hope recalled that Maxine had informed her several times.

The bell rang and Maxine continued, 'That'll be him. He must have worked out that if we're next door to twenty-one and seventeen we can't possibly be sixteen. I suppose it's one way of discouraging any totally moronic visitors, but I really would fix it, Mum, if I were you.'

'Thank you, Maxine, I will.' Hope wondered what she'd done to deserve a daughter so different from her.

A tidiness freak, Maxine couldn't stand things out of place or not working. Her own room was immaculate at all times and she reserved her most expressive sighs for her mother's hit-or-miss style of housekeeping.

She watched now with a disapproving eye as her mother riffled through a pile of papers on the kitchen table.

'Aren't you going to answer it?' she asked, when the bell rang again.

'Could you?' Hope appealed. 'It's a motorcycle courier from one of the ad agencies. He's been sent to pick up some jingles I've written, only I've misplaced them.'

30

'Really, Mum.' Maxine despaired of her mother's inefficiency, before running on, 'He doesn't look much like a courier to me. He doesn't have a helmet, for a start.'

'He'll have left it on his bike,' Hope declared. 'Please, Maxine... before he decides to give up.'

'All right.' Maxine shrugged and disappeared out of the kitchen.

Hope continued searching for the lost music sheets she should have had ready. They represented three days' work and a fairly good commission.

Maxine reappeared. 'He wants to see you, but he's not a courier.'

'Did you ask him who he was?' Hope frowned.

'No, but he looks OK,' Maxine assured her. 'He's wearing a suit and tie and he was fairly polite.'

'Oh, no, he's probably a double-glazing salesman.' Hope had a disproportionately high number of such callers, possibly because the metal window frames of her 1930s semi were so rusted. 'I'm hopeless at getting rid of them.'

'Just tell him we have no money,' Maxine suggested, before wandering back into the sitting-room to rejoin her friend.

Hope raised her eyes at Maxine's comment, and wondered how she was meant to take it. Helpful advice? A statement of fact? A complaint? Or all three?

Years ago, she'd consoled herself that it must be easier to bring up alone a daughter rather than a son. She'd been wrong.

She approached the front door and looked through the opaque glass to find the man still standing on the step, his back to her. She took a deep breath and told herself to be assertive, then opened the door a fraction.

'Look, if it's about the windows, I like them like that,' she said, before the salesman could launch into the usual sales patter.

But it wasn't about windows or doors or insurance or anything safe and boring and ordinary. Hope realised that even before he turned and she saw his face. She recognised him from the back, tall, broad-shouldered, narrow in the hip.

Guy Delacroix wheeled round and stared at her for a moment, long and hard. She stared back, caught by the awful surprise of it. Years stripped away and she felt her treacherous heart flip over at the sight of him.

'You've changed,' he eventually said in his precise, accentless voice, and a shiver ran through her at the sense of *déjà vu*.

She just stopped herself from saying 'you haven't', as her past life ran before her eyes like a drowning man's.

But it was true. He'd hardly changed at all. It had been twelve years since they'd met, yet he seemed little altered. Slightly more grey hairs threaded through the black, and some laughter-lines now fanned from his grey eyes. The latter seemed a strange thing for *him* to have, a man who rarely laughed. Or maybe he had learned how to, since she'd run away from Heron's View—and him.

She thought how different she must look to him. The last time he'd seen her, she'd been only twenty, with the face of a girl and with hair so long it touched her waist. People said she still looked young at thirty-two, but she had the face of a woman, more angular, and her hair had been cropped short. She wasn't at her smartest, either, in jeans and white T-shirt.

'That was your child.' He dragged her back to the present, reminding her that he had just met Maxine.

'I . . .' She wanted to lie, to say no, to deny Maxine's existence but that was absurd. He must have heard of her from Jack. 'Yes . . . Maxine.'

'After your father,' he recalled then commented shortly, 'She looks quite like mine.'

Hope stared back at him, like a rabbit caught in his headlights. He'd noticed the likeness. Of course he'd noticed. How could he not? Apart from her eyes, Maxine was pure Delacroix.

But it was all right. Like his father, he'd said. His father. Jack's father. Same person. She tended to forget. They were so unalike, the brothers.

'I have some news for you,' he went on. 'May I come in?'

She hesitated, wanting to say no again. He didn't give her the chance. He walked past her into the hall. He waited for her to close the door and lead the way.

She avoided the living-room with Maxine in it, and took him to the kitchen.

It was a fair-sized kitchen, with room for a table and chairs.

He stood in the doorway and made it look small. Dressed in a dark lounge suit and conservative tie, he made the room look scruffy too.

'Do you want to sit down?' Hope resented the way he made her feel.

He shook his head. 'This won't take long. As I say, I have some news for you.'

'It's all right. I heard it over the radio,' she informed him.

He looked at her again, as if to gauge her reaction. She lifted her head a little higher, not giving him the satisfaction of seeing she'd been upset.

'And Maxine?' he added shortly.

'I've told her,' she replied just as shortly.

He frowned. 'How is she?'

Hope shrugged. She wasn't going to explain Maxine's feelings to him. He was obviously thinking that the girl who had answered the door to him had scarcely looked grief-stricken, but then what did he expect? He must realise Maxine had barely known Jack.

'Will she want to go to the funeral?' he pursued.

'I—I'm not sure.' Hope hadn't thought that far herself. Jack had only died that morning.

'Will you?' he added.

Her eyes widened in surprise. Surely she wouldn't be welcome—an ex-wife?

'I don't think Jack would have wanted it,' she said eventually.

'No,' he agreed, 'probably not... Is that why you didn't come to my mother's funeral?'

He really hasn't changed, Hope thought as he directed another blunt question at her. He was so different from Jack. It had been 'anything for an easy life' with Jack, but Guy had always met things head-on.

Well, this time, Hope decided, he wasn't going to walk all over her. Her heart might still be racing but her head was clear.

'No, I didn't think *you'd* want it,' she responded sharply.

His eyes narrowed assessingly. 'No, you're right. I wouldn't,' he acknowledged, then added on a note of accusation, 'You came all the same, though, didn't you?'

'What do you mean?' Hope's face went a shade of pink, betraying her.

'I returned to the graveyard after the service,' he informed her. 'I saw you.'

'Oh.' Hope couldn't deny it.

She had kept in touch with Caroline Delacroix even after her split with Jack. Occasionally the older woman would call on her when she was in London. She had come to see Maxine, her only grandchild, but Hope knew she'd never mentioned these visits to her sons.

'Her solicitor telephoned me,' Hope went on to explain, 'saying it was your mother's wish I should be there. So I was... sort of.'

She'd gone down by train to Penzance, then waited until the actual service was over, before going to the graveside. She'd placed an anonymous wreath among the others and said a tearful goodbye to a nice lady.

Hope frowned as she thought of him watching her. What had he felt? Anger, she supposed, that she'd had the nerve to appear.

Guy watched her now, much as he would have done then, with contempt in those wintry grey eyes. 'The solicitor meant for you to come to the house—for the will-reading...' He left the sentence hanging in the air, waiting for her reaction.

Hope didn't rise to the bait. She hadn't expected Caroline to leave her anything, and, if she had, Hope would have heard of it by now. It had been almost two years since Caroline's death.

'Didn't you ever wonder if she left you something?' Guy added at her silence.

'Why should she?' Hope shrugged. 'I wasn't her responsibility.'

'No, you were Jack's.' Grey eyes scanned the room, taking in the state of the kitchen.

Hope wasn't ashamed of her home. It was small and the furniture shabby, but she'd done her best and it was comfortable. The kitchen table and chairs were old and marked, but they were made of solid pine. She had no money for new units but she'd splashed out on some good tiling and wallpaper which she'd hung herself.

But Guy Delacroix was hardly impressed. With a luxury flat in Truro as well as the magnificence of Heron's View, a terraced house in Putney probably seemed one step from poverty to him.

'You didn't get much of a settlement from Jack, did you?' he finally remarked.

She stared back incredulously. He dared say that to her? 'Well, you saw to that, didn't you?' she retorted bitterly.

His brows rose, feigning surprise. 'Perhaps you'd like to explain that remark.'

Hope's lips pursed. He knew well enough. 'Come on. You were the one who advised Jack how little he could get away with. Did you think he wouldn't tell me?'

This time there wasn't a flicker of reaction. Reading anything from Guy's face had always been difficult, and nothing had changed.

'Jack told you I advised him on your settlement,' he stated flatly, rephrasing what she'd just said.

Hope nodded. 'Don't deny it!' she snapped back.

'All right, I won't,' he agreed coolly, his eyes fixed on her face.

Hope refused to be intimidated, and stared back. It was a mistake. She saw reflected in his eyes too many memories, and for a moment felt, as she had all those years ago, that curious mixture of attraction and fear.

She turned away, and started to busy herself in the kitchen, talking to hide her confusion. 'I'll ask Maxine if she wants to go to the funeral. If she does, I'll let you know... Now, if that's all, I have to make tea.'

She ran water into a pan, and banged it noisily on to the cooker, then tried to light the gas with a sparking device. If there was a technique, she seemed to have lost it. She clicked the sparker ineffectively. The smell of gas filled the room.

'The flint's gone,' she was coolly informed.

It did nothing for Hope's humour. She rounded on him, with an idea of telling him to get lost, and they semi-collided as he reached past her to turn off the gas. She grabbed at his arms as she threatened to over-balance, then wished she hadn't. He held her for a moment, and his touch was like a burn on her bare arms. She flinched visibly, and he let her go, but only so that he could turn off the gas. He didn't move away and she was effectively trapped by his proximity.

Hope wasn't frightened of him. She was frightened of betraying herself. Over a decade, but nothing had changed.

He felt her body tremble. His eyes caught hers, trying to see into her very soul.

Appalled by her own weakness, Hope forced herself to remember all of it. Not just the love, but what followed. The hurt. The loss. The ultimate pain of betrayal.

It didn't seem to make any difference: her body continued to tremble at his nearness.

It made no difference to him either, as his hands began to caress her bare skin.

'All this time, and nothing's changed.' He spoke the words in her ear as they stood there, caught by the past.

She shook her head and breathed, 'I hate you,' meaning it.

'And I hate you,' he breathed back, clearly meaning it too.

But he was right. Nothing had changed. Desire was as strong as hate, and just as destructive.

She told herself to break free. She tried to; he held her easily. Not just with his hands but with his eyes. It was strange how such cold grey eyes could be so mesmeric.

'Mum... Mum?' Maxine stood in the doorway, looking from one to the other, unsure what she was witnessing.

At last Hope broke free, almost leaping back from Guy as she caught sight of her daughter. 'I didn't realise you were there,' she said unnecessarily.

Maxine said nothing, but stared hostilely at Guy. He didn't seem to notice, greeting her with a peculiarly soft, 'Hello, Maxine.'

Maxine continued to stare, and Hope stepped in, saying, 'Maxine, this is your uncle——'

'Guy,' Maxine completed for her mother. 'I remember. My father told me about you.'

Not your mother, Guy's eyes said as they slid in accusation to Hope.

Hope's lips tightened. Did he imagine that she had any memories of him which she would willingly share with her child?

His eyes returned to Maxine as he said, 'I'm sorry about your father.'

'Thanks.' Maxine took sympathy from him more readily than from her mother.

'I know he hasn't seen you much lately,' he ran on, 'but he's spent most of the year performing in America.'

'Is that where—where he died?' Maxine asked, a catch in her voice, and, at Guy's nod, added, 'Will he be buried there?'

He shook his head. 'No, we're bringing him home to Cornwall. That's why I've come...to tell you about the funeral arrangements.'

'Do I have to go?' Maxine looked slightly alarmed at the prospect.

Hope decided it was time for her to speak up. 'No, of course not. Only if you want to...'

Maxine still looked uncertain. 'I've never been to a funeral.'

'There's nothing to worry about,' Guy told her quietly. 'It's just...well, a way of saying goodbye.'

'Yes, I suppose.' Maxine accepted his reassurance with a thoughtful nod.

Hope had to give him full marks. For a man without children, he certainly knew how to speak to them.

But perhaps he wasn't—without children. She'd just assumed. Who knew? He might be married, with his own family, by now.

'I can look after Maxine at the service, if that suits you,' he directed at Hope, catching her deepening frown.

'I...um...' Hope looked to her daughter, who gave a nod. 'Yes, OK, if that's possible.'

Hope felt she'd been left with little choice. Maxine had a right to be there if she wanted, and it appeared she did. Her initial hostility towards her uncle had faded rapidly and Hope was left wondering how he'd managed it. She watched them exchanging smiles, acknowledging kinship, and her heart sank a mile.

'Where's Katie?' Hope purposely changed the subject.

'Working in the living-room,' Maxine relayed. 'I came for drinks.'

'All right.' Hope went to the fridge and found two cans of Coke, almost throwing them at her daughter in her hurry to be rid of her.

Thankfully Maxine took the hint.

'See you later,' she said to her uncle, then paused in the doorway to ask, 'Are you staying for tea?'

Hope waited for Guy to give a firm denial. Instead he glanced at her. She didn't have to mouth the word 'no'. Her appalled expression said it all.

'No, but I'll be in touch.' Guy returned Maxine's smile before she disappeared. 'She's beautiful,' he said to Hope, with disconcerting frankness.

Hope felt a moment's pride, quickly followed by guilt, then anger. It hadn't been all her fault. She'd had no choice, and there was no going back.

'Have you any?' she asked in an almost aggressive tone.

He raised a brow. 'Any what?'

Was he being deliberately obtuse? 'Children!'

'No.' He answered her question without giving away any more.

Was he married? Had they decided not to have children? What?

Hope told herself that it was none of her business. A decade had passed and they were strangers. Perhaps they always had been.

Hope was just deciding to steer off personal subjects, when Guy went on the attack, saying, 'I suppose it was worth it—going back to Jack—however temporarily?'

'What?' Hope was taken aback.

'Having Maxine,' he went on relentlessly, his eyes as hard as glass. 'I assume that was the reason for your remarkably brief reconciliation with my brother.'

'How dare you——?' Hope's voice rose with her anger.

'How dare I tell the truth?' he cut across her, at the same time closing the distance between them once more. 'Why not? It hardly matters now. I'm just curious. How long was it, that last time you were reunited? One month? Two?'

Hope was sure he already knew the answer, but she muttered back, 'Five weeks,' and prayed it would shut him up.

It didn't. 'Five weeks?' he echoed, his voice a harsh, mocking sound. 'Let's see, now. Long enough to conceive, have a pregnancy confirmed and get the divorce papers drawn up. Fast going.'

'That's not the way it was!' Hope was more hurt than angry that he could believe that of her. 'I never intended going back to Jack. If you'd just listened to me——'

'Listened to you?' He grabbed her arm when she would have walked away. 'So you could tell me more lies, make more promises you'd never keep?'

'Well, that makes two of us!' Hope remembered all the things he'd said, of love and their future together.

'So maybe we deserved each other.' His lips formed a thin, cruel smile at the idea. 'Maybe you should have stuck with me... But then, you couldn't be quite sure I could give you a baby, could you? Whereas my brother already had——'

'Shut up!' Hope cried at him. 'You and your brother— I was sick of you both. All you ever wanted from me was——' She bit off what she'd been about to say.

But he knew, saying for her, 'Sex?' and laughing his contempt. 'Don't kid yourself. You were never that good.'

'Why, you——' A decade of anger, stored but still festering, spilled over. She raised her hand and slapped him hard on the cheek.

Who was more surprised? Hope, who had never hit anyone in her life, or Guy, who had never been hit?

At any rate, it was Hope who was horrified, who backed away from him, from herself, from the violence of the emotion between them.

It was Guy who seemed almost to relish the situation, as he shot out an arm and dragged her close, forcing her to look up at him, to catch the curious triumph on his face for a moment, confusing her into inaction as he bent his head.

His mouth had covered hers even before she realised his intention. He kissed her hard, branding her as she had branded him, punishing her for daring to slap him.

One kiss and all breath, reason, sanity were knocked from Hope's body. Even as she pushed at his shoulders, kicked at his legs, struggled for her freedom, the most terrible excitement spread through her body.

Guy knew it. He could feel it. That was why he kept kissing her, forcing her lips to open, her mouth, invading, tasting, remembering the sweetness of her, the softness, the smell of her, still the same.

It shocked Hope. Nothing had changed. Guy touched her and she lost all pride, all strength, all will. Guy held her, his hard male hands running over her back, relearning the shape of her as if he had the right. And all the time still kissing her, her cheek, her eyes, her temple, then back to her lips, biting, licking, thrusting into the warm recesses of her mouth until she had to stop herself moaning aloud. But she couldn't stop the memories flooding back, the camera rolling in her head, of him and her, and the time they had loved. The briefest of times, but it was imprinted on her brain as if it had lasted a hundred years.

As were the words he had said afterwards. 'It was nothing. Just sex. Proximity. Curiosity.' And each word had been like a hammer-blow to her heart.

The same words saved her now, dredged up from memory to salvage her pride. They made her cry out, 'No,' and mean it, made her twist from him, with a low curse.

He watched as she wiped her mouth with the back of her hand. It was a gesture of contempt, intended to wound, but the small smile on his mouth mocked her late show of pride.

'I lied,' he said in a low undertone, catching her eyes. 'You were that good.'

It was no compliment. The look on his face told her that was all she'd been good for. A quick session or two in bed.

This time she didn't slap him. Anger gave way to humiliation.

He had the last word, as he'd had the last time they'd met. He turned on his heel and walked away. She heard him go down the hall and open the front door. He didn't slam it.

Guy Delacroix had too much control for such petty gestures. He hadn't kissed her out of desire or impulse. He had wanted to see if he could still reduce her to a weak fool.

He could.

She wrapped her arms round her body. It was still trembling with a mixture of emotions. She felt a little sick. She wanted to go upstairs and lie down and sleep. Sleep for however many days it took to forget Guy Delacroix once more.

But she couldn't. Her daughter trailed into the kitchen, eyes all curious at her flushed face, and she took refuge in her role of mother by busying herself with the tea.

She didn't get away from Guy Delacroix that easily, however, as Maxine insisted on bombarding her with questions about her uncle. What did he do for a living? Did he still live in Cornwall? Was he older or younger than her father? Was he married?

'How should I know?' Hope snapped at the last question as she finally lost patience.

Maxine gave her an offended look, muttering, 'I was only asking.'

'Well, don't!' Hope snapped again. 'Just eat your tea.'

She slapped the plate in front of Maxine and effectively silenced any more talk of Guy Delacroix or the past.

But later, when Maxine went to bed, Hope couldn't silence her thoughts.

Of course, things had turned out just as Guy had predicted. She'd joined Jack on tour in America and it had been a disaster—moving from one American city to the next, living out of suitcases, lying awake and alone in a hotel bedroom while Jack had thrown a party for anyone and everyone next door, still awake and alone the following day while Jack slept off the party.

It would never have been the life for her, but it had been made worse by the depression she was suffering. It had been less than three months since her miscarriage.

Jack, if he'd grieved at all for their dead baby, had long since put it out of his mind. Hope hadn't felt ready for lovemaking, but bare tolerance on Jack's part had quickly turned to resentment. She had given in. Sex had become a joyless physical act without love. Jack hadn't seemed to notice.

She'd been in America a fortnight when she fell ill. She'd felt unwell for days, and had woken up in the early hours with severe pains in her abdomen—and no sign of Jack.

She'd telephoned the hotel reception just before blacking out. A doctor had come. He had called the paramedics, who had whisked her to hospital for a proper examination. It was gynaecological—complications from the stillbirth resulting in possible long-term damage. It was unlikely there would be any more babies.

It had followed the pattern of the stillbirth. Jack had turned up the next day, with flowers and excuses and apparent concern. She had told him that they might never have children now, and he had taken the news almost too well.

He had explained his absence with an all-night poker game, and Hope hadn't challenged it. She'd felt a little guilty herself, because throughout the crisis she had found herself wishing that another man had been there, one who *could* cope, who would be strong, unselfish, reliable.

She'd returned to Britain on discharge from hospital. Jack had made a token effort to talk her out of it, but had been quick enough to arrange for plane reservations.

He'd been less happy with her plan to stay with her friend Vicki until she could find a house of their own in London. Even when not on tour, Jack had preferred to live in hotels, with the convenience of room service, rather than keep a house or flat. He was still trying to dissuade her from her plan as she boarded the plane.

She had phoned Vicki beforehand, of course. Her friend had sounded taken aback at first, then sympathetic at her circumstances. She'd gone on tour with Jack as a gofer the year before, and knew what an exhausting round it was. From her initial reluctance, she'd quickly switched to insistence that Hope make her temporary home with her.

'She's agreed?' Jack said in near-shock when Hope put the telephone down.

Hope nodded, frowning. 'I know you think Vicki is silly and self-centred, but she's not really... You said yourself she was pretty useful as an assistant.'

'Yes, well.' Jack still looked unhappy. 'It's different. You need someone who can look after you.'

Hope shook her head. 'I'll be fine when I get back to Britain, and it'll be less than a month till you join me.'

'I suppose.'

Jack didn't argue further, and Hope assumed the matter was settled. She didn't know Jack very well then. If he wanted something to go his way, he enlisted other people to make sure it did.

In this case, Guy. He was there at Arrivals at Heathrow. But so was Vicki.

Hope noticed them immediately, before they noticed her. It was hardly surprising. They were deep in argument. Guy had his hand on Vicki's arm, holding her there as he talked down at her. Hope was so surprised that she stopped in her tracks and watched. Whatever they were arguing about, it was obviously something heated and personal, yet she couldn't remember any occasion when Guy had even met Vicki.

She was still staring at them when Guy looked up and saw her. So did Vicki, and took a step forward, only to be stopped by something Guy said.

Whatever it was, it must have been something pretty powerful, as the other girl gave Hope an anxious look before suddenly breaking off and almost running in the opposite direction, leaving the field clear for Guy.

He walked up to her, reaching for her hand-luggage, and saying, 'You look exhausted. How are you?'

'I... Fine,' Hope answered automatically, her gaze going beyond him to the milling crowds. Vicki had disappeared. 'What's going on? Where's Vicki gone?'

'Don't worry about her,' he dismissed, and, taking her arm with his free hand, began steering her towards the nearest exit.

Hope went with him rather than cause a scene. She was tired and in no state for a stand-up argument. In the airport bus that took them to the car park, she said with low anger, 'I don't know what you think you're doing, but I've arranged to stay with Vicki and you can't stop me.'

As usual, he kept his cool and replied shortly, 'Vicki's changed her mind.'

'What do you mean?' She just managed to keep her voice down in a bus full of strangers.

'What I said,' he sighed. 'She came to the airport to tell you. I understand there's some man involved.'

'Oh.' Hope stared at him, as if she could gauge the truth of what he was saying that way. He stared right back, his eyes not wavering an inch.

She lapsed into silence. She supposed it was possible. When she'd called Vicki and invited herself to stay, Vicki had initially been reluctant. If she already had some boyfriend staying, that would explain why.

So what was she going to do now? She was still pondering the question when they arrived at the car park and he steered her towards his Jaguar. They'd been travelling for a quarter of an hour before she realised he was driving west on the M4 instead of east towards London.

'Where are we going?' she demanded, although she already suspected the answer.

'To Heron's View,' he said without emotion. 'Jack thought it would be best.'

'What?' Hope struggled to contain her temper.

'Jack thought——' he began to repeat blandly.

'I heard what you said. Stop the car!' she commanded angrily.

'In the fast lane?' He pointed out the fact that they were currently doing eighty miles an hour on the motorway. 'Don't you think that's a bit dramatic? Let's wait till we reach a service station, shall we?'

Hope fumed, but could hardly disagree. Instead she tried to remember if she'd really almost come to liking this man. Briefly. For one day. When she'd been grateful for his coolness, seen it as strength rather than a lack of feeling.

By the time they reached the service station, she'd reverted to disliking him. She didn't get a chance to argue, however, as he installed her at a table, before going off to queue at the counter for coffee. Hope wondered if she could escape then, but, short of begging a lift from a total stranger, she couldn't see how.

He arrived with their coffee, and, before she could go on the attack, he stated his case. 'Jack telephoned me, asking me to come and take you back to Heron's View until he returns. He feels my mother will be much more supportive than Vicki, and I have to agree.'

'I want to live in London,' Hope replied flatly.

'And you probably will,' he countered, 'when Jack finishes this tour. But meantime it would be better if you remain in Cornwall until you're completely well this time.'

Hope wondered if he was doing it deliberately, making her feel like a child who couldn't be trusted to look after herself.

'I think I'll go and phone Vicki,' she announced, her tone defiant.

'Go ahead,' he shrugged, his tone bland, 'although I doubt she'll be home yet... Just don't blame me if you don't like what you hear,' he warned cryptically.

Hope made another face, but sat where she was. He seemed sure of his ground, so presumably Vicki had changed her mind, and Hope didn't fancy being an unwanted third if Vicki had acquired a live-in lover. From memory, she had never really liked Vicki's taste in men.

She felt like crying. Not a very mature response for a married woman, but at nineteen she felt more like a teenager whose boyfriend had dumped her and whose life was falling apart.

She got back in the car with Guy because she could see no alternative, and, despite her resentment and unhappiness, spent most of the journey to Cornwall fast asleep.

When they arrived at Heron's View, Caroline Delacroix was kindness itself. She welcomed Hope like a daughter and, sensing the strain between them, dismissed Guy from the scene.

Hope found herself pouring out her troubles and Caroline listened without taking sides, offering her comfort and support. The older woman had probably known then that Jack wasn't going to change, but she didn't say so. Perhaps she felt Hope needed her dreams of happy-ever-after—at least until she was stronger.

Hope agreed to stay there a month until Jack returned and they found a home of their own. In the end she stayed six, until she realised there would be no home, and no sort of life with Jack, and her dreams had turned to so much dust in her mouth.

Oh, Jack returned. For a few days here and a few there. Long enough to remind her that she was his wife.

Long enough to make her revive the dream a little. Long enough to keep her dutifully waiting.

But in between the loneliness was killing. Caroline tried to help, but Hope was too young for bridge, too old for treats, too married for discos, too single for dinner parties. She helped in the house and spent hours on windowsills reading, and walked the cliffs in the hope that the sharp, clean air would dispel her unhappiness. That was her life, and it felt as if she was slowly dying.

It was Caroline Delacroix who changed it. In the little over a year she had known Hope, she had watched the bright, brilliant blue of her eyes dull to the grey of a winter sky, and couldn't bear it. She meant well. She said that many times afterwards. She set in motion the ultimate break-up of her son's marriage, without any idea of what she was doing.

She had simply thought that Hope needed some social life outside Heron's View, and had recruited Guy to provide it. It had seemed an obvious solution.

Guy could take her sailing with him and his friends. He could take her to the sports club he attended and introduce her round. In between girlfriends, he could surely take her to the theatre.

Her son's reluctance did not discourage Caroline Delacroix. She accepted that he might not like Hope— their relationship was distinctly distant—but he could surely see that the girl was on the verge of a breakdown. Jack's absences were growing longer. Hope's unhappiness was quite evident. They had to do something.

Pressured, Guy agreed, and followed his mother's suggestion the next weekend he was home.

'I have some tickets for a concert a week on Saturday,' he announced over dinner. 'Vivaldi. Would you like to come?'

'I—I...' Hope stared at him in disbelief. The invitation was so completely out of the blue.

'Perhaps classical music isn't to your taste.' He gave her an easy let-out.

She might have taken it, but Caroline intervened with, 'Don't be so patronising, Guy. Hope is quite capable of appreciating fine music.'

'Thanks, but . . .' She searched for another excuse.

'You don't want to go,' Guy supplied for her.

'Guy!' His mother shot him a warning look. 'I realise you're used to instant compliance—not to mention fawning—from your various girlfriends, but Hope doesn't come into that category,' she told him firmly, before turning to Hope. 'At least consider it. You need to get out and about more.'

But not with Guy, Hope decided, and mumbled inadequately, 'I don't know. Jack said he might be able to fly over for a couple of days before his concert in Berlin.'

'And you believed him?' Guy muttered under his breath, but it was audible enough.

'*Guy*!' This time his mother's eyes blazed with anger. He made no apology, his own eyes resting on Hope. Once she would have answered him back, told him to go to hell or whatever. Instead she just sat there, her eyes brimming, as she struggled not to cry.

'I'm sorry. I'm a louse.' He dropped all social pretences as he caught her eye with his.

Caroline Delacroix's breath drew in at her son's admission, even if she heartily complied with his verdict on himself.

But Hope shook her head. 'No, you're right. I don't believe it,' she admitted, and, with a quick, 'Excuse me,' got up from the table.

She felt like running, but somehow she managed to walk towards the dining-room door. She didn't expect either to follow, and certainly not Guy, but he did, catching her up on the stairs. He put a hand on her arm. She turned, ready to lash out at him, but the look of compassion on his face made it impossible.

'I had no right,' he said quietly. 'It's none of my business.'

'I...' His apology was genuine and disarming. 'It is in a way,' she found herself saying. 'I mean, this is your home, and it must be a strain, having a stranger around——'

'It's not that,' he cut across her. 'That's not why. You're not a stranger. You're...'

For once Guy Delacroix sounded uncertain of himself. His eyes searched her face, as if he could find the right words there, but Hope looked back at him in confusion.

'My brother's wife,' he eventually added, as if he really needed to remind himself of the fact, 'and our home is your home.'

The last was said formally rather than warmly, and Hope acknowledged it with a polite, 'Thank you.'

She assumed their conversation was over, but he still had a hand on her arm. She waited for him to release her. He held her for a moment longer, studying her face with his grave grey eyes, and somehow she managed to fight back her tears. He let her go and she walked with dignity all the way up the staircase along to the west wing until she reached her bedroom. Then she flung herself down on the bed and cried like a baby into her pillow.

She cried for the death of her dream. There would be no happy-ever-afters with Jack, no babies, no real family. There would always be tours, concert dates, recording sessions, awards ceremonies—always something that would keep Jack on the move.

Guy had known what it would be like. He had known that first day they'd met and he'd tried to tell her. But she'd been too proud or too stupid to listen. And now it was too late.

She had to accept that this was it. Her life. Her marriage. A few days here and there with Jack, and a lifetime to regret it.

But then, did she deserve any better?

# CHAPTER THREE

A LIFETIME ago. She had been so young. Still believing in fairy-stories. Crying because the big bad wolf Guy Delacroix had been nasty to her. Refusing to admit what was so perfectly plain—that Jack had dumped her there.

'Mother,' a voice interrupted her thoughts.

'Sorry.' She focused on the impatient face of her daughter.

'Can I go and get a Coke or something from the buffet?' Maxine repeated the question she'd already asked, only to find her mother staring into space.

'Yes, all right.' Hope rummaged in her bag for fifty pence, then watched her daughter trailing down the corridor of the train.

What am I doing here? she asked herself once more. Taking a train all the way down to Cornwall for the funeral of a man with whom she'd exchanged only bitter words for a decade.

Not that she was going to go to the funeral. Guy might have bullied her into escorting Maxine. Tied up with all the business of death, he had been unable to come up to London again, and she hadn't needed him to tell her that it was risky for Maxine to travel on her own. But she'd have to go to the funeral on her own; Hope was determined about that.

The funeral was to take place the next morning. Hope would stay in the hotel while Maxine went with her uncle Guy to the church. Then, after the service, they would travel back to London on an evening train. Hope had put her foot down when Maxine had begged to stay for a few days. According to Maxine, Guy had asked them, but Hope doubted it. More likely Maxine had suggested it and Guy had been non-committal.

At any rate, there was no question of staying. This was the end of a chapter of her life. Caroline had died, and now Jack, and there was only Guy left to remind her that she had once been a weak, foolish girl. And he, too, would want to sever the connection forever.

Maybe she could move on now she was free. Arguably she'd been free for a long time: she and Jack had been divorced for ten years. But she hadn't felt it. Every time she'd even come close to forming a deeper relationship with a man, she'd backed away. Perhaps it was fear of another disastrous failure, or perhaps she'd just lost the ability to love.

Whatever it was, she had not been with a man for over twelve years, and, the way she felt, sometimes she wondered if she ever would again. But maybe now...

'You're getting worse.' A voice broke into her thoughts once more.

It was Maxine back again. Hope turned from looking out of the window and looked at her quizzically.

'Worse?'

'Daydreaming. You're always doing it.'

'Am I?' Hope wasn't aware of the fact. 'Well, I'm sure I'm not the only one. Lots of people do,' she added, at the same time wondering why she always ended up defending herself to Maxine.

'Other mothers don't,' Maxine declared with definitive certainty. 'Other mothers get on at their kids for doing it.'

'Probably the same mothers who won't let their kids express an opinion, either,' Hope replied meaningfully.

Maxine wasn't a stupid child. She got the point and pulled a slight face, before shaking her head, acknowledging the futility of trying to improve her mother.

'You didn't give me enough money,' she stated as the reason for her return. 'I need another fifty pence, please.'

'Here.' Hope handed over a pound coin, adding, 'And if I promise to try to stop daydreaming, do you think you could get me a coffee?'

'Sure, Mum.' Maxine shrugged off her mood, and for a moment the love between mother and daughter was silently exchanged in smiles.

Maybe she wasn't much good as a mother, Hope thought, but she wasn't sure Maxine would have fared better with the perfect mother of her imaginings. Maxine longed to be a rebel, and, given a stricter mother, she would have been in her element by now, kicking over the traces with a vengeance.

Not that Hope fooled herself. The teenage years were going to be a nightmare, an impossible task of judging when to insist, where to compromise, and what really was the worst ill. Would it be any better if she had someone with whom to share her problems?

Hope doubted it. She could meet the finest, nicest, most wonderful man in the world, and Maxine would still dislike him on sight. Then it would come down to choices. Maxine would ensure that it did. Me or him? And Hope would make the only choice she could.

She knew all that from experience. There had been Bob, an advertising executive. For a single mum like herself, he'd been a catch. Thirty-five, divorced but childless, attractive—very, funny, kind, good with children. Well, good with children other than hers. She'd seen him at a barbecue, a favourite uncle to his two nieces, but he'd been a non-starter with Maxine. Maxine had declared him 'all right, if you like that sort of person', and made it clear she didn't. Bob had slowly been chilled out of her life, the love he'd professed not strong enough to survive arctic conditions along with celibacy.

Oh, well, Hope sighed rather than wept over her lack of love-life, and dragged her thoughts back to the present. In half an hour she would be in Truro. Guy had promised to arrange a mini-cab to take them to whatever hotel he'd booked. All she had to do was prepare Maxine, mentally and physically, for the funeral, then sit tight until it was over and they could escape back to London. As long as she didn't allow too many more memories head-room, she should survive the experience ...

'There's Uncle Guy!' It was a cry of pleasure from Maxine as they walked along the platform at Truro.

'It can't be, he's——' Hope began to disillusion her, then stopped in mid-sentence as she spotted Guy weaving through the arriving passengers.

Hope's face was a picture of dismay. She had expected to meet Guy just twice more in her life—when he picked up Maxine for the funeral and when he dropped her off. She wasn't prepared for a third time, especially when it came first.

'I had time so I decided to collect you,' he answered her unspoken question in clipped tones, and she wasn't given the chance to argue as he took the bag from her hand.

He led the way, with Maxine at his side. Hope trailed behind. He turned his head a couple of times to check if she was still following, a gesture that did little to conceal his impatience.

Hope wanted to ask him why he'd bothered to come, if his time was so precious, but of course she didn't. She wasn't nineteen any more and allowed to be childish.

She caught up with him as they reached the car park, and he said, 'My car's at the end of the first row. I have to make a telephone call.'

He handed her a set of keys, and walked off. Hope just stopped herself making a face at his back. He'd always been economical with words—unless he wanted something.

'Come on, Mum.' Maxine was already walking down the car park.

For a moment Hope was tempted to escape. They could get a taxi easily enough. The only trouble was that he'd kept hold of her bag.

Another childish idea, she told herself as she reluctantly trailed after Maxine.

Maxine stopped beside a white Mercedes.

'That's not it. His is green.' Hope frowned as she looked across at the next row, trying to find the right car.

'He said the end one, Mum,' Maxine recalled, while Hope realised her mistake.

It had been twelve years since Guy had driven her around in his green Jaguar. He'd probably changed his car four times since then.

Still she was unsure, and the key-ring didn't bear a badge identifying the make of car. 'What if it isn't, and I try and open someone else's car?' she fretted aloud.

'Don't worry, Mum. Look!' Maxine took the keys from her hand and, pointing one at the car, pressed a magic button. The car reacted immediately, kindly unlocking its doors for them.

Maxine gave her a superior smile that said, It's all right, Mum, you don't have to be the smart one in the family.

Hope made a slight face in return, acknowledging her dimness. The whole area of cars, machinery and computers was foreign territory to her, and she was quite happy to keep it that way.

'Wow!' Maxine said, impressed by the car's luxurious interior.

Hope realised then how different life was for Maxine. Hope's father had died broke, but during his lifetime he had earned a fortune and spent it lavishly, and she'd been used to quite a high standard of living. Her own daughter had been brought up on a much tighter budget, and was used to hearing, 'We can't afford it,' from her mother's lips.

She wasn't sure how much Maxine minded. On the occasions Jack had taken her out, it had always been to the best restaurants, followed often by a spending-spree in Harrods.

Hope didn't think he'd done it to be difficult, but it had been exasperating. Once he had kitted Maxine out from head to foot in riding gear, but had never got round to buying the horse he'd promised. Where they might keep it in the middle of London had never occurred to him.

'Is Uncle Guy rich?' Maxine asked outright.

'I don't know,' Hope muttered back. 'Why don't you ask him?'

'OK,' Maxine responded, smiling wickedly as Uncle Guy chose that moment to reappear. She waited until he climbed into the driver's seat, before saying, 'Uncle Guy, I was wondering——'

'*Maxine*!' Hope hissed, unable to believe that a daughter of hers could be so crass.

Guy looked curiously from mother to daughter, while Maxine ran on glibly, 'If I could open a window.'

'Yes, of course,' he responded, his quizzical look now trained solely on Hope.

Hope wondered what was the correct word for the crime of killing a daughter. Daughtericide. It didn't sound right. It was a surprisingly uncommon crime.

'Is there a problem?' Guy finally directed at her.

'All quite normal,' Hope assured him, pursing her lips.

'If you say so,' Guy's eyes rested on her for a moment longer—cool, assessing grey eyes.

Hope looked away. Just twenty-four hours, she reminded herself. She could surely remain detached for that length of time.

Maxine, however, didn't want to remain detached, saying to her uncle when he turned back round, 'Mum thought we had the wrong car.'

'Wrong car?' Guy echoed.

Hope shot daggers at the back of Maxine's head, but to no effect.

'She thought your car was green,' Maxine went on happily.

A silence followed. Hope's eyes met Guy's in the driver's mirror.

'It was—a long time ago,' he said, with a suggestion of a smile in his voice.

Hope looked away first. She didn't want him to know that she remembered, remembered it all.

'How long is it since you and Mum met?' Maxine pursued, oblivious of undercurrents. 'I mean before this week.'

'It'll be thirteen years this September.' He needed no time to calculate it.

Neither did Hope. She was just surprised he knew so exactly. Or did he remember the mess of it all with the same horror?

'Wow, that's a long time.' Maxine made it sound like half a century, before going on even more tactlessly, 'I suppose you weren't likely to meet, after Mum and Dad split up. I mean, you're Dad's brother, not Mum's, so you were bound to take his side.'

'*Maxine*!' Hope didn't so much hiss at her this time as growl.

But Maxine was all innocence as she directed at her mother, 'What?'

In her exasperation, Hope snapped back, 'Could you possibly try putting your brain into gear before you speak? OK?'

Hope rarely became angry. When she did, Maxine had the sense to recognise it.

'OK,' the girl echoed, resentful but compliant.

That might have been the end of it, if Guy hadn't interceded. 'Maxine can say what she likes. It doesn't bother me... The truth is,' he addressed Maxine directly, 'it did put me in a difficult position. Had Jack not been my brother, I would have liked to stay in touch with your mother.'

*Liar*! Hope wanted to scream the word aloud. She wanted to shout at him to stop the car. She wanted to reach forward and hit him, over and over again, until he felt the pain she had suffered then.

Instead she sat in the back of his plush car, curling her nails into her palms, screaming inside, while her whole body went rigid, trying not to betray the fury she felt.

'Oh, well, now Dad's dead...' Maxine trailed off as discretion overcame her natural impulsiveness, and she glanced round at her mother.

But Hope didn't look at her. She stared rigidly out at the passing streets, gradually giving way to Cornish countryside, as they drove to the tip of mainland Britain.

It was Guy who continued the conversation, steering it on to the topic of the funeral, advising Maxine of her part in it. He did it well, Hope had to admit. In quiet, ordinary tones, he was warning her what to expect the next day, so that she would be better able to cope with it.

Perhaps he realised that Maxine was more fragile than her confident manner suggested.

He didn't speak again to Hope until they arrived at the hotel in St Ives. Once booked in at Reception, Maxine immediately disappeared to investigate the leisure club, while Guy ordered tea in the lounge without consulting Hope. She followed him through and sat as stiffly as one could in a plush armchair.

She expected him to discuss arrangements. Instead he remarked, 'Maxine is like you at seventeen.'

Surprised, Hope answered frankly, 'I can't remember ever being that tactless.'

'I don't know.' He smiled a little mockingly. 'I seem to recall your being fairly forthright.'

'I was never——' Hope stopped dead as she saw herself on the verge of walking down memory lane. He waited for her to continue, but she shook her head, switching to saying, 'When should the funeral be over?'

He shrugged. 'Mid-afternoon, I imagine. Don't worry, I will look after her.'

Hope wasn't worried. In something like this, she had confidence in his judgement.

'How upset is she likely to be?' he added neutrally.

'I'm not sure,' Hope admitted. 'She had very ambivalent feelings for Jack.'

'That's hardly surprising.' Guy made a slight face. 'Perhaps you had your reasons, but you did keep Jack away from her for the first ten years of her life.'

Hope took a deep, steadying breath. It was either that or explode.

'Who told you I kept him away? Jack, I suppose?'

'Are you saying it's not true?'

'What do you think?' Hope avoided the question with one of her own.

'I think my brother wasn't too bothered either way,' he conceded bluntly, 'but I know you stopped their meetings last year.'

She had, but only after Jack had failed to appear several times, leaving Maxine distraught. She could have explained this to Guy, but she saw no point. He wanted to believe the worst of her. Let him.

'Are you going to deny it?' he prompted.

'No,' she answered shortly.

'Just as well,' he added. 'I was in Jack's hotel suite when you called. Your voice was loud enough to carry.'

'Really?' Hope tried to look uninterested while she frantically tried to remember what she'd said that time on the phone.

She knew what she'd said later, when she'd visited him at his hotel. It had been the last time they'd seen each other. She'd told him the truth then—or at least part of it—and he had stopped calling.

'You've grown hard,' Guy said, at the lack of emotion in her responses.

Hope agreed. She was surprising herself. Had she really ceased to care?

She shrugged now, as if she was indifferent to his opinion. Maybe she was. Maybe she really had grown hard, grown up, grown able to deal with Guy Delacroix.

Who was she kidding? Her own thoughts mocked her. Deal with him? She couldn't even look him straight in the eye.

She hadn't looked at him directly since the first moment she'd spotted him on the railway platform. She was greatly relieved now when Maxine reappeared to ask if she might go upstairs and watch television in their room.

She saw her chance and stood up, meaning to go with her.

'What time tomorrow will you pick up Maxine?' she directed at Guy, who had also risen to his feet.

'About ten,' he replied shortly, then walked with them towards the lift, taking Hope by surprise as he came up with them.

The key was of the new type, a plastic card slotted in the door. She tried to work it several times before Guy took it from her. He, of course, did it first time. He opened the door for them, then stepped back into the corridor.

'I'll see you tomorrow,' he said to Maxine as she passed him.

'Yes, all right,' a subdued Maxine responded before disappearing into the room.

Guy frowned at her retreating back, then caught Hope's arm as she made to follow. 'There's something I think perhaps you should tell Maxine.'

'Yes?' Hope's brows drew together.

'Jack had a girlfriend,' he informed her abruptly.

'So?' Hope was sure that Jack had had twenty or thirty girlfriends since she'd been his wife.

'A *young* girlfriend.' He grimaced.

That was no big shock to Hope either. She'd worked out long ago that her youth had been part of her attraction for Jack.

'How old was this one?' she threw back. 'Fifteen? Sixteen?'

'Twenty,' he relayed.

'Well! Positively ancient for Jack,' she commented cynically.

His lips thinned, before he continued, 'This girlfriend will be at the funeral. With any luck, I can keep her and Maxine apart, but it might be wise to forewarn her, anyway.

'Yeah, OK.' Hope shrugged.

She knew that what Guy was suggesting made sense, but she wasn't going to thank him for his advice. She wasn't going to thank him for anything.

'Look, I'm trying to make things easier for Maxine,' he clipped back. 'The situation between her parents was hardly her fault, after all.'

'No.' Hope accepted that, but his patronising tone got her back up. 'So tell me, Guy, whose fault was it? No, let me guess. Mine, I suppose.'

'I didn't say that. No one's disputing that Jack treated you like dirt. But then, if you recall, none of us behaved very well...' His eyes raked her face, her body, reminding her just how they'd behaved, before he continued, 'The difference is we were all consenting adults.'

'Shut up!' Hope almost spat at him, not wanting to face the truth that she had, arguably, invited.

'No, this has to be said.' He caught her arm again, when she would have turned away, and forced her to stand where she was. 'All those years ago you made your choice. You went back to my brother's bed and you conceived another child, before deciding to walk out on him.'

'It wasn't like that.' Hope's voice shook with rage and hurt.

'Yes, it was——' He dragged her face nearer his. 'You took him back just so you could dump him. You behaved like a sulky teenager.'

'I *was* a teenager,' she cried back. 'A stupid, trusting idiot of a teenager who didn't know any better. Was that a crime?' Her eyes blazed up at his.

'Maybe not,' he conceded, his voice still vibrating with anger, 'but what you did later was. So you wanted to get back at Jack. Fair enough. So maybe Jack didn't deserve to know his daughter. But what about Maxine? What was it like for her?'

'I—I... You don't know——' Hope tried to defend herself, but he didn't give her a chance.

'I know that a father is better than no father,' he cut across her. 'I know that, however selfish Jack was, he would never have harmed his daughter. And I'm willing to bet Maxine wanted to see him too. But you stopped that, didn't you?'

'You don't know,' Hope repeated, her teeth clenched with the unfairness of it all.

'So tell me!' he demanded, his hands bruising her arms as he held on to her.

Tell him? An angry, irrational part of Hope wanted to. The words came to her lips. It would have been easy. Tell him, and she would be free of the burden. Twelve years she'd carried it. Heavier with each year. Tell him.

'Maxine's not——' She got the first two words out, before she caught up with her own craziness. She couldn't tell him. Not now. It was too late.

'Not what?' His eyes bored into hers, as if he could see into her soul.

But Hope had lost courage. She shook her head, then looked away from him. The fight went out of her.

She finally muttered, 'Not your business,' in a small, defeated voice.

Guy looked down at her face. It was thin and pale, without passion or anger. He realised she had shut down on him. He wanted to shake her, to hit her, anything to bring her back, and for a moment his fingers bit into her arms. Then he pushed her away from him and turned on his heel.

Hope watched him walk down the corridor. She felt no triumph. She felt only shock. She had nearly told him. She had nearly said, Maxine's not Jack's child. She wouldn't have had to say more. Guy was not a stupid man.

# CHAPTER FOUR

'I REALLY don't want to go, Mum,' Maxine said, five minutes before Guy Delacroix was due to collect her.

Hope didn't believe it. Or, at least, she did. It was typical of Maxine.

'You have to,' she said rather snappily, then, hearing herself, added more gently, 'Nervous?'

Maxine nodded. 'Will there be a lot of people there?'

'I don't know,' Hope answered truthfully. 'It's possible. Your dad was very popular. But even if there are Guy will look after you, Maxine, I promise.'

The certainty in her mother's voice didn't totally convince Maxine. 'You say that, but you don't like Guy, do you?'

'I——' Was it that obvious? Hope decided it must be if Maxine had noticed. Normally Maxine only noticed what directly concerned herself. Perhaps she should give her daughter a part-truth, so that she didn't probe any deeper. 'My split with your father soured relations generally with his family. Guy naturally took his side.'

'Did I cause the split, seeing as he didn't like kids much?' Maxine asked in a small voice.

Hope's heart sank. She had thought she'd explained everything so well to Maxine, but it seemed she hadn't.

'No, not at all,' she answered with certainty. 'Your father and I were having problems long before your arrival.'

Maxine looked relieved and Hope was glad, but she didn't feel much better. She told the truth, but only part of it. For twelve years she'd been living a lie, and it became harder, not easier, as time went by.

The telephone rang, a welcome distraction. It was Reception. Guy Delacroix was on his way up.

Hope checked over Maxine. She was wearing a simple navy dress and tights, with flat shoes. It was plain and sober enough for a funeral, even if the girl in them wasn't. With midnight-black hair like her uncle Guy's, and a face like a young Elizabeth Taylor, Maxine was going to be a beautiful woman one day. Already Hope was struggling to keep her a child.

A knock on the door announced Guy's presence, but, even with warning, Hope couldn't control her reaction to him. Even on the day they were burying her ex-husband, she still felt that absurd, painful physical attraction to his younger brother. What love or liking there had been had died a decade ago, yet she still couldn't look at him without remembering.

So she looked away, and crossed to a dressing-table where she had placed a couple of clean handkerchiefs for Maxine.

'Here.' She pressed them into her daughter's hand, then directed at Guy, 'Don't let her get too upset.'

'I won't,' he promised, already placing a protective arm round Maxine's shoulders.

Maxine didn't seem to mind. She accepted Guy as her uncle, although she barely knew him. It was Hope who was the outsider—a silent watcher as they walked along the hotel corridor. Their kinship was evident in their dark hair and dramatic good looks. Their likeness caused her pain and guilt.

Hope tried to recall how much she hated Guy, but the fact was obscured by other emotions. A sense of loss went along with the guilt as she allowed herself to imagine how life might have been. If Guy had meant the things he'd said, if he'd tried to hold her, not let her go back to Jack... If fate had decreed that she met him first.

Hope shook her head over her own foolishness. Jack or Guy, it made no difference. She wasn't destined to be happy with either.

She tried to remember when she'd first known that what she felt for Jack was no longer love—maybe never had been. It was hard to say. For a long time she hadn't let herself be honest. She had kept trying to stay in love, to tell herself he was worth loving, to keep the commitment she had made in her wedding-vows—anything other than face the truth.

But oh, he'd made it hard. And so had Guy...

It had started after that dinner when, cajoled by his mother, Guy had invited her to the concert and she had become upset. To her surprise, he had repeated the invitation several times until she had finally accepted it.

The evening had been a turning-point. Till then, his manner had always been condescending, as if he viewed her as little more than a young girl to be humoured. Although he'd been there when she had given birth, he had gone on regarding her as his brother's child-bride—and something of a family disaster. But that night he had taken her out to the concert he had put his feelings on hold and treated her like a human being.

Hope had responded accordingly, forgetting any enmity, relaxing, talking as an equal, showing an appreciation of classical music that she had learned from her father. It had been a long time since she'd been out and she'd enjoyed herself greatly.

She'd assumed it would be a one-off date but, a week later, he'd invited her to go sailing with some friends of his. She'd been unsure—not having sailed before—but he'd overruled her doubts, saying she could come as a passenger. On the day, however, someone had dropped out and Hope had been recruited as part of the crew.

She had been nervous but Guy had proved a good teacher, patient in the face of her ignorance, and she'd managed to cope even when the weather changed. They'd gone out into the Channel in autumn sunlight, but had returned in a storm. She'd been cold, wet and hungry by the time they'd sailed into shore, but she hadn't complained because she'd felt an odd sense of exhilaration too. She'd discovered a new love—sailing.

After that, he had taken her out with him on his own smaller craft, and, before winter set in, they'd become a competent team.

If they'd kept it to sailing, maybe everything would have been all right. But over the weeks she met many of Guy's fellow weekend sailors, and social invitations started to include her. At first she excused herself on the grounds of expecting Jack home, but after a while it was hard to turn down people without seeming rude.

'We'll be there,' Guy assured one couple when Hope began her usual excuses, and he steered her away before she could say more. 'They've asked you twice now to their house. You can't keep saying no.'

Hope looked at him in surprise. 'I didn't think it was fair. I mean, your having to take me, when you could——'

'Take some beautiful woman more desperate for my company?' he suggested with a wry smile.

Hope gave him a disgruntled look before admitting, 'Something like that.'

'Assuming I can find one, of course,' he said, still with an undercurrent of laughter.

Hope frowned in return, knowing he was teasing her. Caroline Delacroix had made it clear that there was no lack of women in Guy's life.

'Don't worry.' He deliberately misread her expression. 'You may be a bit of a kid, but I can put up with you for an evening.'

'Why, you——' Hope went to hit him, but he dodged her with a laugh. She went for him again, half in temper, half in fun, and he made a grab for her arms, whirling her around until her back was facing him. Then he held her tightly by the waist.

Looking back, that had been the first warning—the first of many she'd ignored. One moment she was struggling in his arms, the next they were both standing still and she was suddenly aware of his breath stirring her hair, of his warmth spreading through the chill of her body.

She was slow to break away? He was slow to let her? Which had it been? She hadn't known then. She didn't know now. It was just something that had happened.

Long ago. To a different person...

'Are you all right?' she asked her daughter when she returned hours later, looking pale and tired.

'Yes, fine,' Maxine assured her, but she didn't quite sound it. 'I'm going to watch TV.'

Hope frowned as her daughter clicked on the television and threw herself down on the bed to stare fixedly at the screen.

Guy motioned for her to come out into the hotel corridor, out of earshot of Maxine.

'There were a few photographers present,' he explained briefly. 'We managed to keep them at bay during the service, but they pursued us to the car. Maxine was a little disconcerted.'

Hope nodded. 'How was she during the service?'

'Weepy,' he admitted, 'but she coped... Better than some,' he added on a slightly acrid note.

'Jack's girlfriend?' Hope guessed, and he gave a nod. 'I did warn Maxine about her.'

'Just as well, because she couldn't have missed her.' He sighed heavily. 'I suspect the lovely Amanda was playing up for the Press. She did everything short of jumping into the grave after Jack.'

His tone was so cynical that Hope found herself defending the girl. 'Maybe she really loved him.'

It drew an even more cynical laugh, before he directed at her, 'You still believe in love?'

Hope assumed it was a rhetorical question and didn't answer. He clearly didn't believe in it, but then he never had.

It surprised her when he went on, 'How *do* you feel?'

She understood what he meant. How did she feel on this day they were burying her first husband—her only husband?

She answered frankly, 'Disconnected . . . It was a long time ago.'

'Yes,' he agreed quietly, 'but *I* still remember.'

He caught and held her eyes for a moment, and the past hung between them, as real as yesterday. She felt herself being compelled to open that box where all secrets and longings had been locked away, but somehow she managed to resist. She closed her eyes and broke the spell.

'I have to pack.' She found safety in the mundane.

'You plan to leave tonight?' Guy queried. 'I booked you in for three nights.'

'Why?' Hope said bluntly, then softened it with a rider of, 'I have to get back. I have an assignment to finish.'

'In that case——' his tone became formal '—I shall inform the lawyer so that you can arrange another date with him.'

'The lawyer?' Hope repeated blankly. 'What lawyer?'

'Jack's,' he replied succinctly. 'He intended to talk to you tomorrow.'

'About what?' Now Hope was suspicious.

He looked at her as if she were playing dense. 'Jack's will.'

'Jack's will?' She echoed his words again, then wished she hadn't. She was beginning to sound stupid. 'He's left something to Maxine,' she concluded, not sure if this was good news or bad.

But Guy shook his head. 'He's left something to *you*.'

'Like hell.' Hope reacted with immediate disbelief, and gave a small, hard laugh.

Guy's face darkened. 'Is it so amazing? You were his wife. You bore him two children.' He made both sound like accusations, as if she had been the one to betray.

'Is this some sort of game?' Hope demanded, sure it must be. 'Because I'm not that stupid, Guy. If Jack had any money—and that's a big if, considering how quickly he used to spend it—I'd be the last person on earth he'd leave it to.'

'It isn't money,' Guy answered flatly.

Hope waited for him to go on. He stayed silent. It *was* a game. He was waiting for her to guess.

But Hope refused to play. 'Well, whatever it is, I don't want it,' she declared, meaning it, 'so if you could just tell the lawyer...'

He shook his head. 'That's not the way these things work. You will have to see the lawyer in person. There are documents to be read and signed.'

Hope sighed impatiently, then a thought struck her. 'Hold on a minute. *You're* Jack's lawyer,' she accused in return.

'I was his business lawyer,' he corrected her. 'I did not deal with his personal affairs.'

'Ever?'

'No.'

'But Jack said...' Hope trailed off as she tried to recall precisely what Jack had said at the time of her divorce settlement. He had maintained that Guy had advised him on his settlement offer, and had claimed she would get no better. At the time she'd accepted the small settlement, feeling she probably didn't deserve more.

'Jack said what?' Guy prompted now.

'Nothing.' She shook her head. How could she prove what the truth was—and did it really matter?

But Guy guessed something of what she was thinking, and ground back, 'You'd still believe Jack over me.'

'No,' Hope countered flatly. 'I'd believe neither of you.'

His eyes narrowed further, but he didn't argue his case. Perhaps he didn't care enough either.

'Jack's lawyer is the family one—Stevens, Stevens and Banks in Truro,' he informed her. 'I'll get Banks to contact you—to relay your good fortune.'

Hope detected sarcasm in his last remark. Was he warning her not to expect much or trying to make her think there was something substantial? Either way, she refused to react.

'All right,' she said coolly, and, intent on ending the conversation, muttered a brief, 'Goodbye.'

'I don't think so,' he contradicted her, just as coolly, warning her that they would meet again.

Hope didn't rise to the bait. She looked at a point past his shoulder, waiting for him to leave.

'I'll expect your call,' he stated on the same cryptic note, before finally walking away.

Her call? About what? Hope was left to wonder. But not for long. The package arrived three days later, by recorded delivery.

She knew what it was even before she saw the heading 'Stevens, Stevens and Banks' on the accompanying letter. The letter told her little other than the fact that she was a beneficiary of her ex-husband's will. The will was enclosed for her perusal.

She read through the usual legal jargon until she arrived at the relevant passage, then, shell-shocked, read no further. She hadn't understood. She couldn't have understood. It was a mistake, a joke, a game. It couldn't possibly be the truth.

She felt no satisfaction. She was too shaken. She went to the telephone. She didn't calculate her actions. She just phoned him.

She got his secretary, who had obviously taken lessons on discouraging unwelcome callers. 'Mr Delacroix is in a meeting.'

'I have to speak to him,' Hope insisted.

'I'm afraid that is impossible at present,' the secretary intoned in her over-refined telephone voice, 'but if you'd like——'

'I need to speak to him *now*!' Hope almost barked at her. 'Tell him it's Hope Delacroix. He'll know what it's about.'

'Delacroix?' The secretary repeated the name, wondering if she'd heard correctly, then gushed on, 'I'm sorry, Mrs Delacroix. I didn't realise. I have only just started work here. I'll get him, of course.'

Hope was left on hold, and given the chance to work out what she planned saying. She wasn't sure. She'd phoned him without thinking. She was just considering ringing off when his voice came over the phone.

'Hello,' he answered shortly.

'Hello, it's Hope,' she returned just as shortly.

'Yes, I had guessed,' he went on drily. 'My new secretary seems to think you're my wife.'

'I didn't tell her that!' Hope denied angrily.

'I didn't imagine you had... Anyway, what can I do for you?' he asked, almost conversationally.

Hope fumed at his coolness. He must know. He was bound to have read the will.

'I've just had a letter from Jack's solicitors,' she announced heavily.

'And his will?' he prompted. 'I did suggest they send a copy.'

'You did?' Hope's tone was incredulous.

'Yes,' he confirmed. 'Is there a problem?'

'Yes,' she snapped back. 'I don't understand it.'

'Really?' His tone became supercilious. 'Well, it's perfectly simple. He left his money to Amanda, the girlfriend. He left his property to you.'

'Jack didn't have any property,' Hope disclaimed, still sure there was a mistake somewhere, or a trick being played.

In the brief time they'd been married, Jack had avoided the purchase of a marital home, and had always stayed at the Ritz or the Savoy when he'd been in London.

There was a moment's silence at the other end of the telephone, as if Guy was puzzling over something too.

'Have you read the entire document?' he finally asked. 'The codicil as well?'

'Codicil?'

'It's a means of adding——'

'I know what a codicil is!' Hope wasn't that stupid, but she could find no such thing as she quickly scanned through the documents. 'There isn't one.'

'That explains it,' Guy said, more to himself than to her.

'Explains what exactly?' Hope prompted.

There was another silence, before Guy informed her, 'Jack had a share in some property in Cornwall.'

'A share?' she quizzed in reply. 'In a hotel or something?'

'Or something,' he echoed unhelpfully.

Hope scowled at her end of the telephone. She could tell Guy was being deliberately obscure, but why? Was he deriving some enjoyment from keeping her guessing?

Well, she was damned if she was going to play along. She didn't believe Jack had left her anything of value, so she wasn't going to get excited about it.

She kept silent, and awarded herself a point when he was forced to continue, 'Do you wish me to explain what?'

Hope was curious, but her pride won out and she matched his coolness. 'Not particularly.'

There was another pause, as if she'd surprised him, before he ran on, 'In that case, I'll leave it to the solicitors. Shall I make an appointment for you?'

'I'll phone them myself,' she said flatly.

'Your choice,' he dismissed, then added, 'Is there anything else?'

What else could there be? Hope might have asked, but restrained herself. It was better that they remain civilised with each other, even if she felt anything but.

'No, thank you,' she said with forced politeness.

'Right, well, I'll get back to my meeting with the managing director of Harko Chemicals International,' he returned in heavily ironic tones, 'and trust he hasn't found a new lawyer in my absence.'

'Oh.' Hope felt a moment's guilt, then shook herself out of it. He was probably making it up. 'Well, give him my apologies,' she added airily.

'I will,' he agreed, before cutting her off with a last, 'See you soon.'

Hope took it as a slip of the tongue—something you might say to any acquaintance. After all, she had no intention of returning to Cornwall, and no plans ever to meet Guy again. She would do what she should have done in the first place—telephone the solicitors.

It was some time before she managed to get hold of Gerry Banks, the solicitor who was dealing with the matter, and, although politer than Guy, he was almost as oblique. Yes, there was an inheritance, detailed in a codicil which unfortunately they had omitted to send. It was impossible to discuss on the phone, however. There were complications. It really was necessary for her to return in person. Perhaps it might be best if she brought her own solicitor.

'I haven't got a solicitor.' Hope had never needed one before. She doubted that she needed one now.

'In that case...' Mr Banks of Stevens, Stevens and Banks paused once more, before saying, 'May I suggest you consider retaining one?'

'But why?' Hope sighed in reply.

'To—um—look after your interests,' he responded carefully. 'Mr Delacroix himself was most anxious that matters should be handled in the correct manner.'

'I don't understand.' Hope shook her head at the telephone. 'Mr Delacroix was... Which Mr Delacroix?'

'Mr Guy, of course,' the solicitor replied, a frown in his voice, before he continued, 'I'm sorry. Did you think I meant...? I should have said.'

'It's all right.' Hope wondered if he thought her mad. Of course he'd meant Guy, but what had it to do with him?

'It is up to you, Mrs Delacroix,' the man ran on more formally, 'but I feel the matter should be dealt with as soon as possible, for all concerned.'

'Yes, fine,' Hope agreed, and promised to ring back to arrange an appointment at her convenience.

Of course, she could have pursued 'the matter' over the telephone, but she didn't feel up to receiving any more surprises and she had a premonition that there was going to be nothing pleasant about this one. Knowing Jack, there would be some catch in it.

She certainly wasn't going to get excited about her so-called inheritance. She hadn't expected anything, and she still didn't. Not that it wouldn't have been nice—a little money to help keep them afloat. Something to enable her to treat Maxine once in a while, instead of always going on about economising... But no, she wasn't going to raise her hopes.

In fact, it all seemed to be a lot of bother as she prepared for a second trip to Cornwall. She didn't wish to take Maxine down there again, which meant finding somebody to look after her for a night.

She went through her list of friends, but there were few whom she saw in the role of babysitter and only one or two who knew Maxine well enough. She telephoned her longest-standing friend, Cathy, only to find her in bed with flu. Another friend couldn't help because she was going away on business. Hope whittled the list down, until she was left with a choice of one—Vicki.

Arguably it was ridiculous that she was still friendly with Vicki, considering all that had happened. But when emotions had cooled and situations had changed, and Vicki's own life had taken a downward turn, they had become friends again. Not great friends. Not see-every-week friends. More friends in a crisis, because they had similar problems. At any rate, she'd long since forgiven Vicki.

Looking back, she wondered if things would have been different had Vicki kept quiet. Some things, maybe, but not Jack and herself. They had been destined for the divorce courts from the day they had married—Vicki had just sped them along a fraction...

Vicki had always been a bit of a coward; she had done it by letter. It had been an over-written letter, as if she had worked on it for hours. Vicki had later confirmed that she had; she had written it one night in an agony of guilt, after a lonely Hope had called from Cornwall and admitted that Jack's absences were fuelling her suspicions that he had someone else.

The letter had arrived on a Friday but Hope had not seen it till night-time. She had spent the day shopping in Truro. Caroline Delacroix had driven her there and they had had lunch together before Caroline had driven on to spend the weekend with a friend in Exeter. Guy had taken Hope home in the evening.

It was nearly Christmas and they had stopped on the way for a meal at a pub restaurant. They'd both laughed a lot, catching the mood of the festive season. By that time Hope had been living at Heron's View for almost six months and she was no longer uptight with Guy. He treated her with the fond indulgence of an older brother, and she followed his lead, playing the rebellious little sister. They argued and fought and yet were surprisingly good friends. Any other feelings for him Hope kept ruthlessly suppressed. She was still ignoring the infrequency of Jack's visits, still waiting for her married life to resume.

It had been the letter that had finally forced her to face up to reality. It had been lying on the mat in the hallway. The eternal optimist, she'd been hoping for a letter from Jack; instead this bombshell had been waiting for her.

At first she'd been pleased. Vicki usually wrote funny letters that cheered her up. She'd carried it through to Caroline's little sitting-room where Guy had lit a fire. She'd sat down to read it while he'd gone to fetch more wood.

She was crying when he reappeared. Crying very quietly while the hand holding the letter shook with shock and anger.

'What's wrong?' Guy asked and, when he didn't get an answer, came to take the letter from her. 'May I?'

She might have refused but she saw no point. She realised Guy probably already knew, had known that day he'd picked her up from Heathrow.

'It's true, isn't it?' She looked up at him and her eyes begged him to be honest with her. No one else had.

He gave a straight nod.

She added, 'Who is he with now?'

This time she half expected him to lie, to protect his brother. Wasn't that what he'd done by turning up at Heathrow and taking her home, rather than risk Vicki confessing earlier?

He answered simply, 'I don't know.'

Hope nodded, accepting it as truth, but she couldn't accept the pity in his eyes. She wiped away the tears that had fallen and stood, straight-backed.

'Excuse me.' She walked towards the door.

'Hope.' He caught her arm. 'What are you going to do?'

'Leave, of course,' she answered with the remnants of her pride. Inside she burned with humiliation.

He caught her other arm and turned her round to face him. 'You can't leave.'

'You can't stop me,' she shot back, angry that he would still support his brother. 'Jack isn't going to care, is he?'

'Maybe not,' he agreed, and, holding her eyes with his, added, 'But I do.'

He said it in such a low voice that Hope wasn't sure if she'd heard or understood. 'What?' she whispered back.

'I care,' he repeated, his face telling her he was deadly serious.

'I—I don't...' Hope trailed off as she wondered what exactly he was saying.

His eyes gave her the answer even before he said quite clearly, 'Come and live with me. Not here. In Truro.'

'Come and live with me.' There was no mistaking what he meant. Her husband's brother was asking her to run off with him. So why wasn't she shocked? Why wasn't she shouting at him? Slapping him? Telling him she wasn't that kind of girl?

Why was she standing there, staring back at him, locked into the most powerful emotion she'd ever felt in her life?

'Jack...' She said her husband's name aloud, hoping it would return her to sanity.

'To hell with Jack!' He almost growled the words back at her. 'He's had his chance. What do *you* want?'

Him. She wanted him. For months she'd hidden from the fact. For months she'd kept reminding herself that Guy was her husband's brother.

'All right, I'll tell you what *I* want,' he continued at her silence. 'I want you. I've always wanted you, right from the first day we met in that London restaurant.'

Hope shook her head. 'You can't have. You were horrible to me.'

'Of course I was!' he threw back at her. 'God, you were too young for *me* let alone Jack... You still are,' he added, seeing her vulnerability written all over her face.

'You *can't* want me!' Hope no longer saw herself as attractive. How could she be when Jack had so quickly turned to someone else?

'Believe me, I've tried not to.' Guy's grip was almost painful as he admitted, 'I've told myself a hundred times it's a passing thing, but it isn't. When you were six months pregnant and looked like hell, I still wanted you.'

'N-no...' Hope was both frightened and excited by his intensity. It was an echo of her own feelings, stifled since the night he'd held her hand and helped her grieve for her dead baby. 'It's not right.' She sought refuge in the impossibility of their situation. 'I'm married.'

'To my brother——' he didn't shy away from the reality of it '—and, if he'd treated you properly, I would have kept quiet. But he hasn't, and it's my turn now.'

There was no doubting the strength of his feelings, no doubting the desire that blazed in eyes she'd once thought the coldest of grey. It drew Hope in until she found herself shutting out everything else.

'Tell me you don't want me,' he urged, even as he took her in his arms.

Hope could have stopped it then. He gave her the chance. She could say she didn't want him and he would back off. It was that simple. It was that hard because she wanted him so badly, it frightened her.

'It's right,' he went on in a low, almost angry tone. 'It's right because I should have met you first, and married you, and given you children.'

The last touched a raw nerve with Hope. There would be no children now, no happy-ever-afters with a faithless husband. There was no future, just the present with this man and the promise of a love that might take away some of the pain.

'Yes.' It was all she said, but it was enough.

He had never kissed her before, but now he took her face in his hands and the mouth that had seemed so thin and cruel at times brushed hers with a tenderness that made tears gather at the back of her eyes. Then his lips opened on hers and spoke of love without saying a word, and her own heart answered, fluttering like a trapped bird, desperate to fly, to escape, to rise and soar to the clouds where her head was already floating. He kissed her harder, bruising, tasting, demanding, his hands moulding her shoulders, her back, restless hands sliding down to her waist, pulling her closer and closer until it was impossible to breathe or think or care if it was wrong.

'Come upstairs,' he whispered against her mouth, and she moaned in assent.

He broke off and took her hand. She went with him, as if she had no will of her own. He switched on no lights. They found their way in the darkness. Up the wide staircase. Along the top corridor to the west wing. To the rooms that had once been hers.

He didn't speak. Perhaps he knew it might break the spell.

Hope was trembling when they reached his bedroom. He drew her inside and shut the door. He left them in darkness as he took her in his arms. He realised their love was too new, too fragile to survive the harshness of bright light.

Hope was hardly dressed for seduction, but it didn't matter. He pulled her polo-necked sweater over her head and unzipped her wool skirt, letting both fall to the ground. She stood in her underwear, too shy, too nervous to undress him. He took off his own shirt. It joined her clothes on the floor.

Guy put her hands on his chest and drew her close to him. The room was cold but his body was warm with muscle and strength. He held her in his arms, the softness of her breasts swelling against his hard, hair-roughened chest. His heart was beating above hers, in a steady, certain rhythm, and she was infused with his vitality. She felt the blood flow through her veins like fire, but she still shivered.

'Don't be scared.' His mouth brushed against her temple. 'We don't have to do anything. I can just hold you.'

Hope shook her head. He didn't understand. It was desire, not fear that made her quiver like a leaf in a gentle breeze. His tenderness overwhelmed her as no force would have done.

'No,' Hope whispered back, her heart in her mouth, but he still didn't understand.

Guy set her from him, thinking she wanted to be free. Hope looked up at him, her eyes now accustomed to the dark, and knew then that she wanted to be tied to this man forever.

'No.' She found the courage to take his hand. 'I need more.'

It was Hope who drew him towards the big oak bed, Hope who parted her lips, waiting for his kiss. Guy was the one to hesitate. He stared down at her lovely, fine-boned face and once more saw vulnerability shading the blue eyes of a young girl. 'Are you sure?'

'I'm sure.' She gave him a small, brave smile that masked any uncertainties.

Perhaps Guy saw through it, his own grey eyes serious and unsmiling, but he had waited many months for this moment. He reached for her, and she went, unresisting, into his arms as they lay down on the bed, mouths seeking, arms caressing, legs entwining.

Hope shut her eyes but the film rolled on. Twelve years later. She could still recall how it had felt, his hard hands on her body, hands both rough and gentle, sliding over the softness of her skin, touching, learning her as if she were an instrument until she had sung for him in sighs and moans. All those empty years, and she could still recall how perfectly they had moved, rising, thrusting, filling as if they'd been made for each other. A lifetime, and she would still hear his sweet, loving lies.

It was what kept her hating.

# CHAPTER FIVE

A WEEKEND, that was all they'd shared before Jack had suddenly appeared, all contrition for his affair with Vicki, begging for a second chance. She'd been so torn, guilty herself now of infidelity, feeling like a hypocrite but unable to face telling him the truth. She had willed Guy to do it, to try to hold on to her, but it seemed his desire for her had died with Jack's return.

What was it Jack had said years later, when he'd finally believed that Maxine wasn't his and had gone on to guess whose she was?

'Well, well, little brother! He always did want my toys.'

It had been said to humiliate, and had been successful, although Hope had long ago figured out Guy's motivation. He'd actually said the words, 'It's my turn now,' moments before he'd taken her upstairs to his bed. She just hadn't wanted to listen.

So, no, she didn't blame Vicki for the whole sorry mess, and, when she'd bumped into her four years later on the London underground, she had not torn her hair out.

By that time, Vicki was in a similar situation, and they were no longer young girls but women with children. Vicki's son, Edward, was a year younger than Maxine. His father had been a struggling musician who had lived off Vicki for a couple of years before running away with an American heiress. Pregnant with Edward at the time, Vicki had had their baby in the vain hope of reclaiming his father. Instead she'd been left like Hope, a single mother struggling to give her child the middle-class background she'd enjoyed herself.

Vicki was more fortunate, in that her parents gave her financial support, but they lived in Cheshire and were too distant to be a practical help. It was Hope who had looked after Edward any time Vicki wanted to go away for a couple of days.

Now it was Vicki's turn to help out and she was willing, if not exactly eager, to do her bit, agreeing to stay the night at Hope's. Long ago Vicki had admitted that motherhood did not come naturally to her, and she could barely cope with Edward, so Hope both threatened and bribed Maxine to be on her best behaviour, and told herself all the way down on the train that nothing too awful could happen in the space of twenty-four hours.

She travelled in the late afternoon, having booked herself into a small hotel in Truro, not far from the solicitors' offices. It was odd to be somewhere without Maxine in tow. She might have enjoyed it, if she had managed to stop worrying about her.

She slept well enough, however, and, with overnight bag in hand, arrived outside the solicitors' doors at nine a.m. for her appointment. She was not on her own.

'What are you doing here?' She did not hide her dismay.

'Nice to see you too,' Guy returned, bland in the face of her animosity. He had obviously been expecting her, his smile a little mocking. He always seemed to have the advantage.

He went ahead of her, then held open the door. Hope didn't feel she had much choice, but decided, once inside, that she'd insist on a private meeting with the solicitor. The secretary at the front desk, however, didn't give her the opportunity, as she showed them both into her boss's office.

'Good of you to come.' Gerry Banks greeted her with a handshake, then waved them both into seats, while he acknowledged her companion with a smile of familiarity. 'Guy—Mr Delacroix—suggested it might be best if he was present to save unnecessary communication through a third party. May I state from the outset that I am acting for the late Jack Delacroix, and no other party?'

Oh, yeah? Hope said to herself, her disbelief mirrored in the glance she gave Guy. She was willing to bet that he and Banks had more than a nodding acquaintance.

The solicitor cleared his throat, as if he was preparing for a speech, before continuing, 'As you probably read in his will, Mr Jack Delacroix left you his property in its entirety. However, as you might appreciate, his being a joint owner of this property makes the whole thing somewhat complicated, as well as the conditions of the codicil.'

'Conditions?' Hope echoed, at the same time wondering what she joint-owned. Knowing Jack, it was probably a casino or nightclub or something on the tacky side of desirable.

Gerry Banks handed her a sheaf of papers which included the will and the missing codicil.

Confronted with legal documents, Hope always felt a little dense. She knew what each individual word meant, but the whole eluded her. It didn't help that Guy's eyes rested on her the whole time she read.

It took her a couple of tries before she made out, 'Jack's left me a house, but only on condition I live there for six months.'

'Well—um—in essence, yes,' Gerry Banks confirmed.

Hope didn't let herself get excited. Knowing Jack, there was bound to be a catch.

'So, where is this house? New York? Paris? Outer Mongolia?'

She'd forgotten that Guy had already told her it was in Cornwall.

Banks didn't answer for a moment. Instead he glanced towards Guy, a question in his eyes, but Guy remained silent.

'I'm sorry. I thought you understood.' Banks addressed her once more. 'The property in question is Heron's View, the Delacroix family home.'

Heron's View! Hope stared at the solicitor in disbelief. Jack had left her Heron's View. Why? How? It had been Caroline Delacroix's and she must have left it to...

Hope finally turned to look at Guy. He was already looking at her, watching for her reaction. She opened her mouth slightly, but her throat was too dry to speak. She tried to tell him with her eyes: she didn't want it; she hadn't asked for it; she knew it wasn't hers.

But Guy continued to stare at her, hard-eyed. He'd known, of course. He'd probably drawn up battle-lines already.

'You are joint owner with Mr Guy Delacroix.' The solicitor stated what she'd finally worked out for herself.

She found her voice. 'I don't understand. Why?' she directed at Guy.

He realised what she was asking and, ignoring the solicitor's presence, answered, 'Maybe you were the love of his life, after all.'

Colour flooded her face at his sarcasm. She glanced at Gerry Banks. He too looked embarrassed.

He cleared his throat once more before continuing, 'It was Mrs Delacroix's wish—the late Mrs Delacroix, I mean—that the house be passed on to you, should Mr Jack die without further issue.'

'Issue?' The term was unfamiliar to Hope.

'Children,' Guy put in shortly, making her feel her ignorance.

'I did explain to both parties that this might cause problems,' the solicitor said, excusing himself from any responsibility for their current situation, 'but they were determined. Should you live there for the required period, of course, it becomes somewhat simpler. Your name would go on the title-deed and then it would be a matter of coming to an agreement with Guy, should you wish to realise your equity in the property. You understand?'

'Vaguely.' Hope understood that, if she were to profit from her inheritance, it would be up to Guy.

It was he who put the options to her. 'You can either sell your half to me, buy my half from me, persuade me to sell along with you, or wait for me to die and persuade my beneficiaries to do one of the three.'

Hope shook her head. None of this was relevant, as she would never be inheriting. 'I'll make it simpler. No, thanks.'

She rose from her chair, ready to leave.

'Mrs Delacroix?' Banks looked baffled by her move.

Guy was less surprised. He stood up with her, letting her pass him on her way to the door.

'Mrs Delacroix?' Banks called out to her, but she kept walking.

'I'll handle it,' Guy assured him as he followed her out of the door.

Hope kept walking until she was out of the solicitors' offices and halfway down the road. She knew Guy was shadowing her, and she eventually halted and turned to say, 'You don't have to "handle" anything. I'm giving it to you. Heron's View. Free of charge.'

He caught her arm when she would have walked away from him. 'Well, that's good of you,' he said, his tone saying the opposite, 'but right at the moment it's not yours to give. And we have to talk,' he added, taking her overnight bag from her hand.

'Where are we going?' she demanded as he propelled her across the street.

'In here.' He pushed her inside a pub on the corner, and installed her in a corner booth of the lounge bar. 'What would you like to drink?'

'It's a bit early,' she pointed out.

Not surprisingly, they were the pub's only customers.

'So? Pretend it's later,' he suggested drily, and went off to the bar.

He returned with a lager and whisky for himself, and a bacardi and Coke for her. It was what she used to drink as a teenager. Nowadays she preferred a dry white wine.

'Have a drink.' He put the glass in her hand. 'It'll help you get over the shock.'

Hope grimaced, wondering if he was being sarcastic. He was right, however. She did feel shaken. She took a gulp of her drink, hoping it might steady her nerves for what was to come.

'I suppose you knew all about Jack's will,' she accused, forgetting for a moment that it was hardly to his advantage either.

'As a matter of fact, no,' he denied coolly. 'I knew, of course, that my mother intended him to leave his share of Heron's View to you or Maxine, but, as it was more a moral than legal commitment, I imagined Jack would ignore it.'

'You hoped he would, you mean,' she returned tartly, sure he felt as she did—trapped in an absurd situation.

He shrugged, as if it had been a matter of little importance to him. 'Wherever he left it, it was going to be a problem for me.'

'Well, it isn't any more,' Hope pointed out, 'because I won't be staying at Heron's View for six months and therefore I won't be inheriting.'

'Really.' He was unimpressed.

'I mean it,' she insisted fiercely.

'That's your choice——' his composure was still irritatingly perfect '—but if I were you I'd give yourself time to think about what you're doing. It's not just you, remember. There's Maxine.'

Hope frowned. 'What has Maxine got to do with it?'

'Jack hasn't left her anything directly,' he pointed out, 'but, through you, he has... Do you know how much Heron's View is worth?'

Hope shrugged. She refused even to speculate. She wasn't going to live there, and that was final.

'Jack had it valued two years ago on our mother's death,' Guy went on. 'A conservative estimate is one million.'

Hope, who'd been taking a sip of her drink, nearly spluttered into the glass. Heron's View might be a big house with a unique location, but she'd never dreamed it would be worth so much.

Guy registered her reaction. 'Does that change things?'

Hope shook her head before saying, 'I don't understand you. Why are you telling me all this? You can't want me to inherit, when it could all be yours.'

'If you don't inherit, then someone else does,' he amplified. 'Not me.'

'Oh.' Hope had assumed it all reverted back to him. She recalled now that she'd read only one paragraph of the codicil in the solicitor's office. 'Then who?'

'The lovely Amanda,' he said scathingly.

Jack's last girlfriend, Hope recalled. She'd seen a photograph of her in a tabloid after the funeral. She had looked lovely, but vacuous. Is that how she herself had first seemed to Guy?

'Well, does it matter to you which of us gets it?' she asked, making a slight face.

'Of course it does.' His tone implied she was being fatuous. 'For a start, Heron's View is my home, and I don't relish the idea of sharing it with some brainless bimbo Jack picked up in a disco. For another, that house has been in my family for a hundred years and I'd sooner keep it that way.'

Hope frowned in surprise. Obviously he didn't consider *her* family, but he must regard Maxine as such.

'Look, I'll tell you straight,' he continued at her silence. 'Should you inherit, I won't be able to buy you out. Not at a fair price. I could raise about three hundred thousand, but that's all... I assume you'd be in a similar position with regard to buying me out.'

Hope gave a short laugh. 'Right at the moment, I couldn't raise three thousand.'

'OK.' He took it as support for his argument. 'And the way things are set up, as joint owners neither of us may sell to a third party without the other's agreement. In no circumstances am I prepared to sell Heron's View. So you see the position?'

Hope wasn't sure she did. 'If I were to inherit,' she deliberated, 'I couldn't sell unless it was to you, and you couldn't afford to buy, so I would never gain any benefit from owning Heron's View, unless I were to live in it on a permanent basis, which I'd never do.'

'No, you won't benefit,' he confirmed, 'but Maxine will. One day she'll own Heron's View.'

'Half of it,' she corrected him.

He shook his head. 'No, all of it . . . I intend to leave her my share, should you inherit.'

Hope stared at him, round-eyed. He was kidding. He had to be. He would leave half of a house worth one million to a child he hardly knew?

She protested in disbelief, 'But what if . . .? When you have your own children . . . You can't possibly——'

'I won't have children,' he dismissed with utter certainty.

Hope shook her head. 'You can't be that sure.'

'I won't marry, not now,' he said, as if the chance of it had passed him by, 'and I don't believe in having children outside marriage. I practise safe sex so there will be no accidents.'

'*What*?' His bluntness made Hope gasp.

'I said I——' he started to repeat.

'I heard,' Hope cut him off, before her face went any redder. Did he have to be so frank? She wondered how he'd like it if she was equally frank back, and reminded him of a time he hadn't practised what he preached. A time that had resulted in 'issue', as the solicitor had termed it.

'So, you can see,' he went on blandly, 'it may not be to your advantage, but it is most definitely to Maxine's.'

Yes. Hope could see that. She just didn't trust that he was doing this for Maxine.

'Is this Amanda so awful?' she enquired cynically.

'Absolutely indescribable.' He grimaced in distaste. 'So you'll do it?'

'How can I?' Hope appealed. 'My work's in London. If I lose my contacts, even for six months, I'd have to start again and it's my only source of income.'

'I thought you wrote jingles for commercials,' he said in a dismissive tone.

Hope resented his critical air. OK, so composing jingles wasn't vital, life-enhancing work, but it had enabled her to pay a mortgage and bring up Maxine.

'What I mean is,' he added on a more conciliatory note, 'surely you can do the same in Cornwall? Land's End it might be, but we do have telephones, fax machines and even the odd tape recorder. You could put your material on tape and send it.'

'I have to liaise with advertising executives,' she pointed out.

'So?' He gave her an impatient look. 'You can always go up on the train—or even fly.'

'I can just imagine how much flying would cost,' she muttered back.

'I'll give you the money, if it's a problem,' he offered, but out of exasperation rather than generosity.

Hope pursed her lips. All right, so she might be able to solve her work problems, but what about Maxine?

'There's Maxine's schooling,' she argued. 'It would be disruptive for her.'

'I don't see why.' He sighed at her obstructiveness. 'There are schools down here, and she's nowhere near her exam years, is she?'

'No, but...' She searched for other reasons. 'It's not easy for children, switching schools mid-year, then being expected to switch back just six months later. Maxine would miss her friends and it's not so easy to make new ones when you're twelve, especially if you have a different accent——'

'I'm sure Maxine makes friends very easily,' he concluded, quite correctly, 'and, from talking to her, she doesn't seem too keen on the school she presently attends.'

'What do you mean?' Hope demanded crossly.

'Simply what Maxine has told me,' he responded, 'and typical of a city comprehensive, I should imagine. Disaffected pupils. Disaffected staff. And precious little discipline.'

Hope's lips tightened at his description. Clever as she was, Hope doubted Maxine had used the word 'disaffected'. But she hesitated to defend the school, when she wasn't particularly happy with it herself.

'Well, where did you expect me to send her—Cheltenham Ladies' College?' she asked defensively. 'And which bank do you suggest I rob to pay for it?'

'You could have asked Jack,' he pointed out. 'She was his daughter as well.'

Hope's face went a betraying pink but he didn't seem to notice, as he continued, 'Anyway, the obvious thing to do is ask Maxine.'

'Ask her?' she echoed in surprise.

'Why not?' he argued. 'She's the one a move would affect most, but she's also the one who stands to gain the most. So why not let her decide?'

Hope could think of one very good reason. Maxine might just think it a wonderful idea. And that would put her in the most impossible of positions. Refuse, and she would be cheating her daughter of a sizeable inheritance. Accept, and she would have to live with a man she found unbearable, in a house that now held only painful memories for her.

'I have to think about all this.' Hope played for time.

'Fair enough,' he conceded. 'How long are you staying in Truro?'

She shook her head. 'I'm not. I stayed last night. I have to return today.'

'Where's Maxine? Back at the hotel?' he enquired.

'No, she stayed in London with a friend,' she said somewhat hesitantly. She didn't want him knowing who the friend was.

His eyes narrowed in speculation. 'Friend? Male or female?'

'Does it matter?' she said, even more cagily.

'Not really,' he shrugged. 'I just wondered if a boy-friend was behind your reluctance to come down to Cornwall for six months.'

Hope's eyes went to his as she wondered if he could be so naïve. Didn't he know *he* was the reason she didn't want to spend one minute more than she had to round here? Apparently not.

'Should I take your silence for assent?' he resumed, a mocking edge to his voice.

'Of course I have a boyfriend. Several, in fact,' she claimed extravagantly. 'Don't you know? Men just posi-tively queue up to date single mothers over thirty!' she rattled back, and, leaving him to read her answer how he liked, added, 'So, if you don't mind, I have a train to catch.'

'I'll come with you.' He rose and took her hold-all from her hand, following her out of the pub. 'I might as well speak to Maxine immediately.'

Hope halted on the pavement and didn't hide her dislike of the idea, snapping back, 'Don't you have any work to do?'

'Not today,' he responded. 'I've taken the day off.'

Hope's eyes narrowed on him. 'You had all this planned, didn't you? Before we even met the solicitor?'

'Naturally.' He didn't even try to deny it. 'Is that so surprising?'

'Surprising, no. Sneaky, yes,' Hope retorted.

He raised a brow at her choice of word, then shrugged off any insult. 'Heron's View has been my home since I was a boy. I'd like to keep it.'

It was a plain statement of fact, not an emotional appeal, but it still made Hope stop and think. Till then she hadn't really thought of things from his perspective. Now that she did, she saw that he might have some cause for complaint.

Heron's View had been owned outright by his mother, and she could have left it solely to him, but she must have felt obliged to divide it equally. But there was no argument who had been the better son.

'Have you to go back to your hotel?' Guy's voice broke into her thoughts.

'No.' She had paid the bill on leaving.

'OK, my car's just round the corner. I'll leave it at the station.' He waited for her to fall in step beside him.

Hope sighed resignedly. She supposed it would be easier to sort everything out today. Last week she'd insisted on going back to London, and it had led her to make an extra, unnecessary journey. If she refused to let Guy accompany her now, it just meant that he'd turn up in London some other time, and it would be worse because she wouldn't be expecting him. This way she was at least forewarned.

At the station he ignored her protests and upgraded her ticket to first-class. They had few fellow passengers in the carriage. They sat opposite each other and talked little. He read *The Times* from cover to cover while she tried to concentrate on the novel she'd bought.

Hope's thoughts, however, kept straying to Maxine and her possible reaction to the news. Would a future inheritance mean anything to her? She supposed it would, and wouldn't that be natural? She had got used to living on a tight budget and long ago accepted it, but Maxine was at the beginning of her life, and the promise of a fortune, albeit many years away and dependent on the death of an uncle who might live to a hundred, might be hard to resist. Yet part of her hoped she would resist it, and choose to make her own way in the world.

At one o'clock they went to lunch in the dining-car. Hope would have preferred a sandwich, but Guy had made reservations and it was easier to go along with him than argue.

'Are you going to eat that?' Guy broke into her thoughts and made her realise she'd just been shoving her spaghetti round the plate with a fork.

'I'd sooner not.' She had no appetite.

'No wonder you're so thin,' he commented, pushing away his own empty plate.

'I've always been thin,' Hope declared heavily.

'No, you haven't.' He let his eyes travel down her body, then return to hold hers.

Hope found herself colouring, knowing they were sharing the same thoughts. He'd had first-hand knowledge of her body and she hadn't been thin then. Her first pregnancy had turned her figure from a girl's to a woman's, and, unlike Jack, Guy had appreciated her fuller breasts and curving hips.

'I suppose your boyfriend likes you like this,' he added, his eyes speculative now.

What boyfriend? Hope could have said, but she wouldn't give him the satisfaction. It was none of his business.

'Could we possibly talk about something else?' she said instead.

'All right.' A shrug dismissed the subject of her love-life, and he went on, 'Do you still sing?'

'Sing?' she echoed, not following.

'I understood you worked as a backing vocalist at a recording studio,' he relayed, to her surprise.

'That was years ago.' It had been almost five years since she'd done such work. It had been quite well-paid but very erratic, and her jingle-writing fitted in better with her role as single mother. 'Who told you that—Jack?'

He shook his head. 'My mother—after one of her meetings with you in London.'

Hope's jaw dropped. 'I thought...'

'She kept them secret?' His smile mocked her as he revealed, 'She did from Jack, but she had no idea you might be unmentionable to me too.'

He caught her eye for a moment but Hope refused to return his stare. He seemed to be accusing her of something, yet surely neither of them had been a saint. He'd wanted her, and he'd had her. She'd wanted—comfort? Love? A shoulder to cry on? She wasn't sure which any more. But they had both used each other, and she was the one who'd paid the higher price.

'She worried about you a lot, you know,' he continued, at her silence. 'She thought the Delacroix family had ruined your life.'

'Really?' Hope wondered why he was telling her all this. She kept her eyes on the passing scenery as the train sped them to London.

'I said you were tougher than that,' he went on inexorably, and smiled slightly as that succeeded in drawing her attention back to him. 'Were you?'

Hope wasn't sure what he wanted to hear. That he and his big brother *had* ruined her life? That they had both broken her heart? That they'd left her so messed up she hadn't been able to love another man since, either physically or emotionally? Was that what he wanted to hear?

'Much tougher,' she answered him in a hard, flippant voice, and was proud of herself for doing so. He was never going to know the pain he'd caused her.

'That's what I thought.' He looked at her with an oddly ambivalent look, as if he both admired and disliked her. Then he asked out of nowhere, 'So, when exactly did you tell Jack about us?'

'I—I...' The colour drained from Hope's face. 'I never actually told——'

He cut across her, 'Last year, wasn't it?'

He was right. Jack had found out last year, but she hadn't intentionally told him.

When the novelty of having a beautiful daughter had worn off, Jack had started breaking promises to Maxine. Arranging to take her out and not turning up. Offering to buy something and then simply forgetting. Hope had recognised the pattern and watched helplessly as Maxine began to wonder why her dad no longer wanted to see her. The final straw had been the school concert. Jack had promised to be there to hear Maxine sing a solo; there had been no sign of him, and no word, and Maxine herself had declared that she never wanted to see her father again.

It was Hope who had gone up to meet him the next time he was staying at the Savoy. She had told him how Maxine felt, but it hadn't worried him. He'd been sure that Maxine would see him again, especially as he planned to take her on a shopping trip. It was then that Hope had realised she had to do something before Jack spent the next ten years breezing in and out of Maxine's life, with his destructive mixture of charm and ruthlessness.

She had told him straight. Maxine wasn't his. He hadn't believed her, not at first. How could Maxine not be his when she was so much like his own father? Coincidence, Hope had claimed. But Jack had still refused to believe her. Who else could she have been with at the time? She'd been stuck in Cornwall.

And then it had struck him: how Maxine could be like his father; where Hope had been staying at the time; who else had been around while he'd been absent.

'Well, well,' he had said with scorn, 'little brother! He always did want my toys.'

Hope had said nothing, but he'd been sure. Her silence had been as good as a confirmation. She'd left when he'd started throwing at her words like 'whore' and 'bitch'. It seemed that he'd forgotten his own infidelity.

She'd lived in dread for weeks, expecting Guy to come knocking on her door, but there had been nothing.

'What did Jack say?' she asked him now.

'Nothing directly,' he replied. 'It just became obvious that he knew you and I . . . Oh, there were no pistols at dawn or sword-fights on the battlements. In fact, I think he rather enjoyed the situation.'

Just as Guy seemed to be enjoying the situation now, Hope read in the half-smile on his face. He was enjoying raking up the past to make her feel uncomfortable—and to make the point that neither he nor Jack had taken *her* too seriously.

Well, she wasn't going to add to his pleasure, Hope decided as she declined to offer any comment.

It didn't discourage him, as he speculated aloud, 'Hence the codicil, I suspect.'

'The codicil?' Hope's curiosity got the better of her. 'You mean the bit about me having to live at Heron's View for six months?'

He nodded. 'He's probably looking down on us now— or in Jack's case up—and having a good old laugh at our expense,' Guy suggested in ironical tones, then added more darkly, 'A final act of vengeance, perhaps, as he watches us tear each other apart.'

The last chilled Hope, unsure whether it was a threat on his part or just an assumption of the inevitable. Whichever, she couldn't believe it was some grand plan of Jack's.

'Isn't that all rather fanciful?' she challenged coldly, not letting him see that he was making any impression on her. 'If Jack was after some sort of revenge, he wouldn't have waited until he died. That might have happened forty years from now.'

Guy looked steadily at her for a long moment, before he said, 'I don't think so.'

At first Hope took him to mean that, with his life-style, Jack had never been going to live to be an old man. Then she saw in his face some knowledge that he was keeping from her.

'How did Jack die exactly?' She had understood it had been in a car accident.

'He was driving while drunk,' he responded bluntly. 'He crashed into a tree.'

Hope wasn't too surprised. She'd only lived with Jack a couple of years, but it had been long enough to recognise his dependency on alcohol.

But still she sensed that Guy Delacroix was keeping something to himself. She might have pursued it, but he didn't give her a chance.

He signalled the waiter and, when she refused a dessert, requested the bill. They returned to their carriage and silence descended once more.

Hope made no attempt to break it. On reflection, she didn't really want to know Jack's motives or the circumstances leading up to his death. She wanted to be free of the past: Jack, and the man sitting opposite her who had broken her heart all those years ago.

# CHAPTER SIX

'WHAT time does Maxine come home?' Guy enquired when the taxi caught at St Pancras finally deposited them outside her home.

'In an hour or so,' Hope calculated, then, because she could do little else, said, 'You'd better come in.'

'As an alternative to sitting on the doorstep, you mean?' he returned drily.

Hope pursed her lips. She seemed to be doing that a lot lately. She unlocked her front door and, collecting the day's mail from the mat, trailed through to the kitchen. He followed.

It was a mistake. She'd forgotten Vicki's untidiness. One day, and she'd managed to make the kitchen look a tip. Dirty plates from breakfast still lay on the table. Pans, presumably from last night's meal, sat on the cooker.

She glanced in distaste at the mess, but resented it when she caught Guy wearing exactly the same expression.

'Not very domesticated, your boyfriend, is he?' he remarked sarcastically. 'Smoker, too, I see.'

He spoke with the disapproval of a man who was both obsessively tidy and physically fit. His words struck chords that Hope would rather not have touched. Maxine also turned up her nose at Vicki's slovenly ways and bad habits.

'There are worse faults,' Hope snapped back as she started to clear the dishes.

'So I see.' He picked up a cigarette stub from the ashtray. 'Wears lipstick too, does he—this boyfriend?'

Hope gritted her teeth to stop herself saying anything too rude.

'There's no boyfriend,' she admitted, just to shut him up. 'A female friend of mine looked after Maxine.'

'Really?' He raised a questioning brow. 'How interesting. Now I wonder why you told me otherwise!'

'I didn't!' Hope claimed quite correctly. 'You assumed otherwise.'

'And you let me,' he concluded. 'Did you think you'd be safe that way?'

'Safe?' She gave him a blank look before carrying the dishes to the sink.

He was undeterred, following her as she almost threw them into the bowl. 'Safe from my advances.'

From being irritated, Hope stepped over the line to being infuriated, and she rounded on him. 'Hardly! I mean, it didn't bloody bother you before that I was married.'

The words flew out of her mouth. She hadn't planned them. But they must have been there in her head.

They had the desired effect, too, as they wiped the arrogant half-smile off his face. The look of cold fury that replaced it, however, made Hope lose courage.

He grabbed at her arm before she could walk away from him, and grated back, 'You're wrong. It bothered me all right. It bothered me beforehand when I lusted after my brother's wife; it bothered me afterwards when you went running back to him, still warm from my bed.'

'Don't!' Hope tried to twist free from his grip and, in doing so, dislodged a pan that was sitting on the drainer. It fell to the floor with a loud bang.

They both stared at it for a instant. The noise made them take a pace back.

'Let me go,' Hope instructed in a voice tight with control.

And he did, dropping his hands away. He looked neither embarrassed nor apologetic, saying simply, 'We seem to be living up to Jack's expectations.'

Hope understood. Not a day in each other's company, and they were already tearing each other apart. Was that really what Jack had hoped for?

'This is impossible.' Hope shook her head. 'I couldn't live at Heron's View for six hours, far less six months.'

'You have to.' He spoke as if it was a fate neither could escape.

'No. No, I don't.' Hope shook her head again and, with a husky appeal of, 'Please go, Guy,' she turned from him and left the room.

She went upstairs and sat down on her bed. She didn't worry that he might pursue her. For some reason she trusted him to leave of his own accord.

That was before the doorbell rang. It rang just once and Hope half wondered if she'd imagined it. By the time she walked out to the landing to lean over the banister, Guy was opening the door and it was too late.

She couldn't see Vicki, but she could hear her. 'Oh, hello... It's Guy, isn't it? Is Hope back?'

'Yes, she's upstairs,' he answered slowly, as if he was puzzling over something.

'Well, if she's resting, tell her everything's fine,' Vicki ran on, 'and I just came back for my bag.'

Hope remained where she was, listening to the exchange of voices. She figured there was a chance, if she stayed up here, that they would both go away.

Eventually she heard the door shut, then nothing. Assuming Guy had departed with Vicki, she breathed a sigh of relief and took a couple of steps downstairs. She froze when she saw him still in the hall, then turned tail when he noticed her.

Only now he no longer felt like respecting her privacy. Instead, he took the steps two at a time, and opened her bedroom door just seconds after she'd shut it behind her.

She tried righteous indignation, spluttering at him, 'What do you think you're doing? Get out of my room! I've asked you to leave——'

'And I will,' he threw back, 'when you've explained what that cow was doing here.'

'Cow?' Hope still considered indignation her best bet. 'If by that you mean my friend——'

'*Friend*!' He snarled the word back at her, and advanced to where she stood by the window. He stopped a little short of her and struggled to contain his temper as he bit out, 'Correct me if I'm wrong, but wasn't that one Vicki Martin? Your old school friend? Also known as your husband's lover and author of the true confessions of a slut?'

Hope breathed deeply to control her own temper. She didn't know why *he* was so mad at Vicki. It was her business if she'd chosen to forgive her.

'What if it is?' Hope clenched and unclenched her hands, wanting to hit him.

'You let that woman take care of your daughter!' he accused in disbelief.

'Why not?' she flared in return. 'For God's sake, she's not an axe-murderess.'

'*She... slept... with... your... husband.*' He emphasised each word as if she needed reminding.

'She and a thousand others,' Hope cried back. 'What do you expect me to do? Persecute her for her stupidity? I was guilty of that myself, remember!'

'I'm not likely to forget,' he ground out.

'What?' Hope knew it was an accusation without understanding it.

'How do you think I felt when you went back to him?' His voice was taut with fury.

'I have no idea.' Hope refused to answer him, refused to look at him as she turned to gaze out of the window.

He closed the gap between them and, grabbing her arm, forced her round to face him. 'Then I'll tell you how I felt. I felt like someone had put a knife into my guts and ripped them out,' he told her graphically. 'I felt that way every day you remained with him. And every night I shut my eyes and saw you with him. His hands all over you. His mouth on yours——'

'Don't!' Hope couldn't listen, wouldn't listen as she broke free once more and covered her ears with her hands. But he dragged her arms away and, pushing her backwards, trapped her against the wall next to her bed.

'His mouth on yours...' Hoarsely he whispered the words in her ear. 'Touching your cheek, your throat. His mouth on your breast——'

'Stop it!' Hope cried out desperately.

But relentlessly he went on, 'His mouth where my mouth had been. And all the time I could see the look on your face, hear those little panting noises you make——'

'Shut up! Shut up! Shut up!' Hope repeated wildly as he opened wounds that she had thought healed over.

They hadn't been. She too could see it as he did, only it wasn't Jack making slow, wonderful love to her, but this man, all those years ago, whispering words of love in her ear, making her believe, making her want, turning her inside out as Jack never had.

He was still whispering, only the words were curses now. Yet it made no difference. As he held her to him, his body trapping hers, she felt the same longing for him, and it shamed her. Even as tears filled her eyes, her body trembled for his touch. And the worst thing was that he knew it.

His lips ceased moving to form words, and instead they stirred against her hair. She went on trembling as they pressed to her temple, before moving in a slow trail to her mouth.

She opened her lips to say, *Please don't,* but the words were lost against his—and she was lost the moment he began to kiss her.

Lightly at first, then more insistently, he pressed his mouth to hers while his hands caressed her arms, her back, her thighs.

Desire was like a drug, a rush of sweet agony that frightened her with its intensity. She tried to save herself. She pushed at his shoulders, even as she went on tasting him as he tasted her. She pushed harder as she felt herself losing herself in him.

He broke off the kiss and, raising his head, looked down at her. He knew. He saw it in her unfocused eyes. He heard it in the breath she could barely catch. He knew she wanted him as he wanted her, and that was all that mattered to him.

He held her eyes with his and drew her down on the bed with him. Hope felt her own will slipping away. When he started kissing her again, she could no longer remember why she needed to stop him. He pressed her back against the satin of her bedspread and she opened her mouth to his. They kissed over and over, as if that might be enough for them.

But it wasn't. He rolled over on to his side and took her with him, his mouth still fastened to hers. He kissed her more gently now, as a hand followed the curve of her hip, upwards to her neck. Then he broke off the kiss and began unbuttoning the blouse she wore. He took his time, his fingers brushing her skin, his eyes holding hers once more.

Hope was shaking by the time he'd finished. It had been thirteen years since she'd been intimate with a man—this man. She both longed for his touch and dreaded it. When her blouse was open, he drew one side off her shoulder and down her arm. All the time he watched her face until eventually she had to look away.

It was then that he touched her, re-learning her body as his hand moved downwards from the soft skin at her neck to smooth over the rise of her breast. But he was in no hurry. He kissed her face, her eyes, her cheek, her mouth as his fingers returned to trace the fine bones at her shoulder. He knew exactly what he was doing. He was making her wait, making her ache—for him, for his touch, for the hand that finally pushed aside her underwear and reached to cup her breast, his thumb circling to find its swollen peak.

She stifled a moan as his fingers stroked her, then cried aloud when he suddenly bent his head and took a nipple in his mouth. He sucked hard on her flesh until desire became overpowering. She did not resist as his hands dragged her blouse and bra off. She no longer cared if it was right or wrong. She wanted him as she had wanted no one else.

She lay there, waiting, when he raised himself away and discarded his own shirt. She lay there, letting him, as he unzipped her skirt and pushed first it, then her tights, down over her hips. She shivered a little, whether from cold or nerves was uncertain, but he lay back down on the bed with her and drew her into the circle of his arms. Her breasts touched his bare chest and she felt the warmth of his body spread to hers, and the taste of him was like sweet wine on her tongue as he kissed her once more.

She forgot who he was, who she was, and why they should hate. It was hard to remember when it seemed more like love, his mouth covering hers, a kiss that both gave and demanded, travelling downwards, in a slow trail, her breasts, her nipples, in his mouth, his clever, knowing mouth. His hand was moving downwards too. Spreading. The flat of her stomach, then inside the lace of her pants. Already moist. Wanting. Needing. Opening for him. Touching her. Stroking. Clever, knowing fingers. Breath in gasps. Quicker. Harder. Harder to breathe. No more. Crying. Crying out his name. Endless. Over.

Then there was the awful part, the part where breath slowed and flesh cooled and sanity returned, bringing with it the shame and guilt. But not for him. He had been in control, had always been in control, was in control now as he sat, still clothed apart from his shirt, watching her.

It had all been planned. He had meant to do this. He had meant to make her want him, want him so much that she would let him touch, take, brand. Not willing to make love to her properly, he had still left his mark, on her, inside her, visible to his cold grey eyes.

She turned away, clutched the bedcover to her nakedness and hoped he would just go. But his games were not over yet. He lay back on the bed with her, and started to kiss her back, her shoulders, to run his hands down her body.

Hope was appalled. Her skin trembled at his touch. The ache started again. How could she still desire him? He had just humiliated her. How could she possibly still want him? Yet she did.

'Hope.' His hand curved on her naked shoulder, gently persuasive, wanting her to turn to him. When she resisted, he touched his lips to her back and said, 'It's all right. I can wait.'

Hope did not respond. She couldn't. Her pride was dust in her mouth. He thought she was so easy that he could have her any time.

She heard him get up from the bed, then heard another noise. It took her a moment to identify it. Someone was knocking at the door. Someone was calling through the letterbox. The front door was just below her bedroom.

'It's Maxine,' Guy said unnecessarily as she sat bolt upright on the bed. 'I'll answer it... Perhaps you'd better put some clothes on,' he added, his eyes resting on her naked breast, half exposed by the cover she clutched.

It was ridiculously late for modesty, but Hope's face still flooded with embarrassment. He stared a little longer while he buttoned up his own shirt, then, with a last remark of, 'I'll tell her you're taking a shower,' sauntered almost casually out of the door.

The moment he was gone, she sprang into action. It was hard to know what to do first. She threw her blouse and skirt into the linen-basket. She collected fresh clothes from the wardrobe. She dumped them on the floor while she desperately straightened out the bedcovers. Then, clothes in hand, she dashed to the bathroom and locked the door.

She turned on the shower and half waited for Maxine to come upstairs. But she didn't. Obviously Guy was a greater attraction.

Well, she supposed she should understand that. She had not been able to resist him herself.

For thirteen years she'd lived without physical intimacy. It hadn't been so hard. She'd had boyfriends but none she'd liked, or loved, enough to sleep with. One had suggested she was under-sexed and Hope had wondered if it was possible. Now she wished it were.

She stood under the shower, and soaped off all traces of sweat and sex, but couldn't wash away the memory of his touch or the hard, unpalatable truth. She had enjoyed it, every minute of it. He had told her no lies about love. He hadn't spoken at all. He had serviced her like a stud and she had cried out for him, when, emotionally, he had been a million miles away. That was what was so humiliating.

It would never happen again, she promised her reflection as she tried to hide the damage under a heavy layer of make-up. She wouldn't let it happen again. He could wait all right. He could wait until hell froze over.

Maybe he wouldn't care one way or the other, Hope thought as she finally went downstairs to find Maxine chatting nineteen to the dozen with him. He was as cool as ever. So cool she might have convinced herself nothing had happened, if there hadn't been the merest suggestion of a smile playing on his lips every time he looked at her.

She did her best not to look at him as Maxine acknowledged her presence with a list of complaints against Vicki.

'Honestly, Mum——' she sighed heavily '—she hasn't a clue. Do you know what time she made us go to bed?'

'Nine?' Hope suggested, not sure if she was up to this conversation.

'No,' Maxine dismissed. 'The point is, she didn't. She didn't say a word. It was eleven before I decided to go myself and that monster Edward was still running around.'

'Who's Edward?' Guy put in.

'Her progeny.' Maxine had learned the word in biology just that day.

'Vicki's married?' Guy directed at Hope.

She shook her head.

It was Maxine who insisted on answering more fully, 'Edward is the product of a failed love-affair. That's how Vicki describes him,' she justified at Hope's quelling look, 'and in front of him, too. No wonder he's disturbed.'

'Maxine!' Hope gave her another look.

Maxine responded with the charm she could turn off and on like a tap, 'Well, all I can say, Mum, is I'm glad I'm *your* daughter.'

It was accompanied by a sweet smile which didn't take Hope in either, but she laughed all the same, forgetting their audience for a second.

She caught his expression. He was smiling too, but there was mockery in his eyes. It made her think once more of what had occurred upstairs, and she flushed in embarrassment, wishing he'd just go. For a moment she wondered if he might say something to Maxine, then realised she was being absurd. What was he likely to say? That he'd enjoyed having sex with her mother this afternoon? Even he wouldn't be that crass.

Instead he carried on chatting to Maxine, asking about school. She was suitably scathing and Guy laughed at her account of her eccentric biology teacher, telling her about his own experience of a less than normal geography master he'd had at school. They chatted easily, as if they knew each other well, and Hope stood by the sink, watching, as if she were the outsider. When he glanced back in her direction, she gave him a look of enmity.

It prompted him to get to the point of his visit. 'Maxine, there's something we have to tell you about your father's estate.'

'Estate?' Maxine didn't understand, but she was worried by the sudden switch to seriousness. She glanced towards her mother but Hope decided to leave it to Guy to explain.

'His will,' he continued levelly. 'Your father didn't leave you anything directly, but he did your mother. He has deeded her half of Heron's View, the family home in Cornwall, on condition that she lives there for a minimum of six months.'

Maxine's face cleared. She obviously didn't find the prospect alarming.

'You mean—we have to go and live down in Cornwall? Wow! Great! Is it by the sea?'

Guy nodded. 'It overlooks the Atlantic Ocean.'

Maxine smiled again, then frowned as another thought occurred to her. 'What happens after six months? Do we come back here?'

'Yes,' came from Hope.

'But why? Do we have to?' Maxine appealed to Guy. 'I mean, if we like it and it's half our house, why can't we live in it always?'

'In theory, you could,' he responded, drawing an exasperated glance from Hope. Did he have to encourage Maxine? But maybe she was being unfair to him, as he added, 'However, that is your mother's decision.'

'Mum——' Maxine turned to her '—when can we go?'

'I don't know.' Hope tried and failed to keep irritation out of her voice. 'You can't just leave school in the middle of term.'

'There's only two weeks to the summer hols,' Maxine countered.

Hope hadn't realised it was that close. The holidays were always an awkward time for her. It was difficult to work with Maxine around the house, and normally she had only sufficient funds to take her for a week's bed and breakfast in Brighton.

'It'll be brill.' Maxine was jumping ahead of her. 'The whole summer in Cornwall. We'll be able to go swimming and riding and all sorts. Uncle Guy's got a sailing boat, haven't you?'

Uncle Guy nodded, his eyes on Hope as he said, 'Your mother used to enjoy sailing. She was quite good at it, as I remember.'

'Were you, Mum?' Maxine's tone was surprised. She rarely considered her mother outside the context of their current lives.

Hope shrugged and breathed deeply to contain her anger. Guy might have sold Maxine on the idea but it wasn't going to be anything other than a prison sentence to her.

'I could teach you,' he continued to Maxine, 'like I taught your mother.'

'Would you, Uncle Guy?' Maxine's excitement was evident.

Guy smiled back at her with what seemed like genuine affection. Perhaps it was, but it made Hope feel no better.

At last Maxine noticed her lack of enthusiasm, appealing, 'It'll be fun, Mum, and you'll be much better off, won't you, owning another house?'

Hope didn't know how to answer this question. She didn't really want to go into the financial aspects of it.

Guy had no such reticence. 'Not really. She won't be able to sell unless it's to me, and I'm afraid I can't afford to buy.'

'Oh.' Maxine absorbed this thoughtfully, while Hope shook her head slightly at Guy, not wishing him to add anything about the possibility of Maxine's inheriting the whole house.

It wasn't that she didn't trust Guy's intentions. Perhaps he did regard Maxine as his natural heir, but there was still time for him to marry and start a family of his own. She didn't want Maxine building her life on expectations that were both distant and uncertain.

'Never mind.' Maxine shrugged off any difficulties. 'We can still go for six months, can't we, Mum?'

Hope wanted to say no. So what if it cost her the inheritance? She was used to a moderate lifestyle now, and it might be better for Maxine if she too had to make it on her own.

But it was hard to say no when her daughter's eyes were on her, large and blue, and pleading like a half-starved puppy's. Her thoughts weren't on inheritance or money, but on a fairy-tale house that stood at the top of a cliff looking out across the sea.

'All right.' Hope finally gave way for the simple reason that she wanted to make her daughter happy.

From Maxine's look of delight, she'd succeeded.

Guy looked pleased too, as well he might. Six months of inconvenience, then he'd have a lifelong and solitary occupancy of Heron's View.

'When?' Maxine pressed once more.

Hope shook her head, and it was Guy who said, 'Maxine, give your mother time to make plans... Within the month, shall we say?' he directed at Hope.

'Yes, all right,' she agreed stiffly as he rose from the table.

'See you soon, Maxine.' He gave her a smile before following Hope out of the room.

She went to the front door and held it open for him, bristling with resentment. As usual, he had got what he wanted.

Aware of her feelings, he said in almost conciliatory tones, 'You're doing the right thing.'

'Possibly,' she agreed shortly. 'Just don't expect me to be happy about it.'

He heard the hard note in her voice but he still smiled, a thin, speculative smile. 'Actually, I never know what to expect from you, Hope. You can be spitting fury at me one moment, and the next... Well, take what happened earlier.'

When she'd been a push-over, he meant, and Hope itched to slap the arrogant, self-satisfied look off his face. But that was what he wanted. He wanted to see her lose her cool, admit that he'd got to her.

'What happened earlier?' she echoed, as if she had to dredge her memory for it. 'Oh, you mean in my bedroom. Well, let's not make too much of it. It's a couple of months since I broke off with my last boy-friend,' she said with studied nonchalance.

He flinched—physically flinched. Hope felt good about it.

It was her turn to smile. She even managed to keep smiling as he returned harshly, 'Jack said you'd turned into a slut. I should have believed him.'

He obviously believed his brother now. The contempt in his eyes was absolute. But Hope didn't let it get to her. At least, not until he turned on his heel and slammed the door behind him, and then he wasn't there to witness her pride collapsing as she realised how foolish she'd been.

She had wanted to put him in his place, to dismiss his importance, but what a way to do it. Making out she slept around, when she'd only ever been with two men in her life. It was stupid.

Or maybe it wasn't, if it kept him from touching her again. That was what she wanted, wasn't it?

Yes, her head said loudly and firmly. No, came from another part of her that felt rather than thought, that longed, and needed—and had to be stifled before it tore her apart a second time.

# CHAPTER SEVEN

'IT'S ab fab!' Maxine declared two weeks later, the morning after they had moved into Heron's View.

'"Ab fab"?' Hope prayed it was teenage jargon for awful.

'Absolutely fabulous,' a grinning Maxine disillusioned her.

'Oh,' Hope sighed, but couldn't argue with her.

They had arrived late the night before, too late to see anything and too tired to do anything but crawl into bed. Now it was morning and, with the sunlight streaming through every window, Heron's View really was every bit as beautiful as she remembered.

Maxine's room was big and bright and indisputably better than her room in London. It had a splendid view over the cliffs and the bay below, with the Atlantic stretching endlessly. It had masses of cupboard space for clothes, and shelves for books, with colours and soft furnishings that were bold and modern and practical. It looked as if it had been decorated with a young girl in mind.

Hope had to console herself with other drawbacks. Maxine had no friends here and no way of making them until school started. There were no ice-rinks or cinemas or video shops within a bus ride. There were no boutiques for an increasingly clothes-conscious girl to scour. Surely Maxine would be bored and begging to return after a month or two?

'Everything OK?' Guy asked when he appeared in the room, followed by a red setter.

'Fine,' Hope said tightly as she continued to unpack cases and hang up clothes.

'It's ab fab,' Maxine repeated the latest slang as she knelt to hug the tail-wagging setter.

Guy lifted a brow at Hope. 'Is that good or bad?'

'Good,' honesty made Hope admit.

'Well, anything she doesn't like she can change,' he offered generously.

'Thanks.' Maxine smiled up at her uncle.

Hope didn't. She looked as cross as she felt.

'Is there a problem?' he asked, when Maxine walked through to inspect her adjoining bathroom.

'No, not if you like spoilt children,' she retorted heavily.

'I'm only trying to make her—both of you—feel welcome,' he defended himself.

Hope's expression changed to disbelief. 'Isn't that rather risky? Make us too comfortable and you may not be able to shift us when the time's up.'

Her tone was more mocking than serious. She assumed he was being sarcastic too, in responding, 'Maybe I won't want to shift you.'

Hope didn't retaliate. If they weren't careful, they'd end up spending the next six months in one continuous quarrel.

Thankfully, Maxine returned to reclaim his attention. 'Can I swim down there?' She pointed at the bay below the cliffs.

'Yes,' came from Guy.

'No,' cried Hope simultaneously.

She glared at him. He ignored her, addressing Maxine instead. 'You can swim down there, but only with adult supervision. All right?'

'Yes.'

'Promise!' he insisted.

Maxine nodded and repeated solemnly, 'I promise.'

Hope stood there, a spectator, made to feel redundant. He was taking over, just as he had done all those years ago. He'd taken her over from Jack, then dumped her flat.

'We'll go swimming later,' he suggested, and it drew an eager smile from Maxine.

Hope wondered how long it would be before Maxine reverted to her normal, uncooperative self. She felt she would prefer it to this model of obedience put on for Guy's benefit.

It continued through lunch. There was no, 'Yuck, vegetables!' when Guy put both broccoli and carrots on her plate.

The meal had been prepared by a Mrs Stevenson from the village, who cooked and did some light housework for him. The heavier cleaning was done by another woman.

Hope was going to have little to do round the house and it felt odd, after years of running her own house, to be waited upon.

'That was good,' Maxine declared after demolishing a syrup sponge for dessert, then added disloyally, 'Mum doesn't cook puddings, not proper ones.'

Hope glared at her, but couldn't really argue the point. Syrup sponge—or any sponge for that matter—was outside her culinary range. Normally dessert was a choice of yoghurt or fruit.

She imagined Guy might make capital of her short-comings, but he seemed to be more intent on being conciliatory.

'Your mum has her work,' he said to Maxine in mild reproof.

Maxine looked a little sheepish. 'Yes, of course.' She gave her mother a smile of apology. 'But that means it'll be good if Mrs Stevenson does all the cooking. You'll manage to get lots done.'

'I imagine Mrs Stevenson is only here at weekends,' said Hope, 'when your... Guy is home.'

'Oh, I forgot,' Maxine directed at Guy. 'Mum says you live in Truro during the week.'

'I used to.' His eyes went to Hope rather than her daughter.

'*Used to*?' Hope's heart sank.

'Didn't I say?' He was all bland innocence, knowing perfectly well that he hadn't said anything. In fact, Hope had asked if he still had the flat in Truro and he had said yes. 'With fax machines and computers and suchlike,' he went on, 'I can do most of my business from home. I still have an office in Truro, but I'm only there a couple of days a week.'

And the rest of the time? Hope was horrified as she realised that the rest of the time he'd be hanging around Heron's View.

'You said you still had your flat.' Her tone was accusing.

'I do,' he claimed, 'but I rent it out. Short holiday lets, mostly.'

He smiled as if they were having a normal conversation. It took all Hope's restraint not to shout, Liar! at him across the table.

'But that's great, Mum,' an oblivious Maxine declared. 'We'll see much more of Uncle Guy than you thought.'

'Great,' Hope echoed in a voice so deadpan that Guy actually laughed.

Maxine looked quizzical and Guy said, 'I think your mother's struggling to contain her enthusiasm.'

Maxine didn't really understand, but she laughed along with Guy.

Hope wondered, was she being paranoid, or was her daughter aware of the underlying enmity and was rapidly choosing sides? Not her mother's, of course. Guy was a much more interesting prospect.

Guy was certainly going out of his way to make Maxine's stay pleasant. He took her swimming after they had digested their lunch and didn't reappear for hours.

Hope was invited too, out of politeness, and she declined without considering it. She made an excuse about working, then spent much of the afternoon on a window-seat overlooking the ocean, thinking of everything but the best tune to sell a fat-free sausage that tasted disgusting. It was quite an opportunity for her—a jingle aimed at a television audience rather than just radio. But its importance did nothing for her concentration.

She ended up following the urge she'd had since arriving the night before. Guy had come to London for them and their belongings, and, with motorway delays on a Friday night, it had been a long, exhausting journey. But her eyes were still drawn to the tower in the west wing where she had lived during her very first stay at Heron's View and where later she had gone with Guy and lain in his arms when she'd discovered that Jack had betrayed her.

She didn't know why she needed to see the tower. It wasn't going to help her bury the past. It wasn't going to make her feel better. But she felt compelled.

It was as she remembered. If it had been repainted or wallpapered, it was in the same style as before. The furniture was the same, too. She looked to the bed and had a vivid memory of them lying there together. They hadn't just made love. They had talked for hours, as new lovers did, confessing hopes and dreams, admitting failings.

She wondered now how she could have been so naïve. Guy had wanted her because she belonged to his brother. But he had only made love to her to prove that he could have her.

She had hated him for that. She had hated him more than she ever had Jack. She had seen Jack for what he was—weak, self-centred, an incomplete character who was driven by the latest impulse. But Guy always knew exactly what he was doing. He was in control, a planner, a calculator, a man who had no weaknesses.

She watched from the tower window as he arrived back with Maxine in the MG sports car he kept for summer use. She could see her daughter smiling, happy, looking across at her 'uncle' with admiration. Was that part of Guy's plan, to keep in with Maxine by playing the father-figure? The irony of it made Hope feel sick rather than

amused. She hurried back to her room in the east wing
before she could be discovered where she shouldn't be.

'I think he's got a girlfriend,' Maxine announced as she
entered her mother's room like a whirlwind.

'What?' Hope looked up from her pretence of working
on the music-sheets scattered on her bed.

'Uncle Guy,' Maxine said, as if she thought her mother
slow. 'I think he's got a girlfriend. Well, I know he has.
We met her in St Ives.'

'Really?' Hope tried to sound uninterested while she
sorted out her true reaction. Her stomach was in knots.
'What were you doing in St Ives?'

'Uncle Guy took me swimming near there,' Maxine
explained, 'then he offered me an ice-cream.'

'Don't you think you're too old for ice-creams?' Hope
snapped in irritation, then wished she could take the
words back.

Maxine was quick to capitalise on them. 'You're
always telling me that I'm only twelve and I shouldn't
be in a hurry to grow up! Now you're saying——'

'Yes, I know,' Hope cut in, 'and I'm sorry... I guess
I'm just a little on edge.'

Maxine decided to be gracious and accepted her
apology with a sympathetic, 'Is it work? Isn't it going
well?'

'Not very,' Hope admitted, rather than tell her the
truth. She was finding her daughter's growing relationship with her real father hard to reconcile herself
to.

'I'm not surprised. They taste like rubber gloves.'
Maxine had been her guinea-pig for the new sausages.

Hope wondered how Maxine knew what rubber gloves
tasted like, but decided not to ask.

Unfortunately, Maxine switched right back to earlier
topics. 'Her name's Elizabeth. Very tall and elegant, but
quite old. Older than you, even, I think.'

'*That* old!' Hope widened her eyes in mock-horror, having been made to feel one step away from her pension, then exercised considerable self-control by not asking about this Elizabeth.

She didn't need to ask, however. Maxine was happy to trot out, 'Rich, though. You could tell from her clothes... He's taking her out tonight, so we'll be on our own,' she added, down in the mouth.

'Don't expect Guy to take you out too often, Maxine,' her mother warned quietly. 'He does have his own life.'

Maxine made a slight face, then brightened up with, 'He's taking us out tomorrow. Lunch at the yacht club.'

'Really?' Hope assumed 'us' would be just Maxine, and felt a mixture of things.

Maxine obviously liked Guy and wanted his company. Perhaps the feeling was mutual, and what harm could it do? But she remembered Jack sailing back into their life, raising Maxine's expectations, only to let her down. Hope had seen it as damaging for Maxine and had been quite ruthless in getting rid of him. Should she be the same now?

It was a moral dilemma, harder in some ways than it had been with Jack. He had treated Maxine badly and he'd had, in Hope's eyes, no right to keep seeing her. But Guy was different. He was treating Maxine like a favourite niece, and Hope had no fears that he would let her down as Jack had. Also he was her father, a fact Hope couldn't ignore no matter how she tried. The burden seemed greater now that the two had met, and she could see no way of getting rid of it. She would have to live with this terrible lie, day in, day out, until they returned to London six months later.

Maxine was correct. Guy went out to dinner and Hope told herself she was glad. One less meal to suffer. One less hour to stand being with a man who made her angry just by being near.

'Why not?' he asked her at breakfast the following morning, when she declined his lunch invitation.

'I have work to do.' She gave the simplest excuse but her hostile glance told him the real reason.

'On the glorification of sausages?' he said, very tongue-in-cheek.

Hope might have cheerfully strangled Maxine if she hadn't already left the kitchen table to walk Rufus, Guy's dog.

'Sounds fascinating,' he added in a patronising tone that had her curling her fingers into her palms.

'No, it's bloody boring!' she snapped back. 'But it pays for the clothes on Maxine's back and the food in her stomach, and I'm not going to apologise for it.'

She pushed her coffee-cup away, still full, and would have risen if he hadn't reached out to clamp a hand on her wrist.

'Let me go!' she spat, failing to twist free.

'In a second.' He continued to hold on to her. 'I want to apologise first.'

'*Apologise*?' Her tone was one of disbelief.

'I was being condescending,' he admitted, 'about your work. As you say, it's enabled you and Maxine to survive... It just seems a waste of your talents.'

'My talents?' Hope looked suspicious.

'As well as possessing a more than adequate singing voice, you can compose music and lyrics,' he recounted. 'Once you planned on being a songwriter, remember?'

Oh, she remembered. It was when they had been lovers. She had confessed her dreams to him, half expecting him to laugh. Instead he'd insisted on hearing the three or four songs she'd written, and had been warm in his approval. Later she'd assumed he'd been flattering her for his own reasons. Whichever it was, she had ceased writing love-songs before Maxine's birth.

'And you planned on sailing the Atlantic single-handed,' she point out.

'True,' he conceded with a wry smile, 'and maybe I never will now. But I still dream of it. What about you?'

Hope returned his stare for a moment. Did he really care about whether she had dreams any more? She shook her head at the absurdity of the conversation.

'I have no dreams,' she stated flatly. 'Now, if you'll excuse me...' She looked pointedly down at the long fingers still circling her wrist.

He relaxed his hold, and she jerked her hand free. She walked to the door and his voice stopped her this time as he asked, 'Do you mind if I take Maxine to lunch?'

'What if I say, Yes, I do mind?' she countered, feeling bloody-minded.

'Then I won't,' he replied simply.

Hope had expected an argument. His reasonableness wrong-footed her.

'Take her if you want,' she muttered, and left the room before she gave way to the urge to pick another fight with him.

She watched him leave with Maxine a few hours later. They were dressed casually in summer sailing clothes of navy and white. Looking at their thick black wavy hair and similar features, she wondered if outsiders would recognise the truth. Would they think what a handsome pair father and daughter made? Would they guess her secret?

Hope knew it was possible, yet she'd made no attempt to stop Maxine going. To have done so would have been to deliberately keep her from her father, and Hope didn't want to do that. Circumstances had led her to bring up Maxine on her own, and if she had lied by omission it was because she had believed it the best thing for Maxine. Jack had assumed Maxine was his, but hadn't wanted her, not until she'd grown to a civilised age. Hope had assumed that brother Guy would not have wanted a baby either, and she had not invited a second rejection.

She told herself she had not been wrong. She told herself that Guy's interest in Maxine was solely con-

nected with Heron's View. If he kept Maxine happy, the
girl would want to remain in Cornwall, at least for six
months, and, in her turn, would pressure Hope to
remain. Hope couldn't afford to believe that he was
genuinely fond of children, couldn't let herself contemplate that he might have wanted a share in his baby
daughter. It was too late now.

Hope was playing the piano in the drawing-room when
they returned hours later. She stopped at the sound of
voices in the hall and went out to greet Maxine. She was
not alone, but with another girl of roughly the same age.

'Hi, Mum, this is Natalie,' she introduced the girl as
they headed for the staircase. 'We're going to listen to
my tapes.'

'Oh, hello.' Hope exchanged brief smiles with Natalie
before they disappeared upstairs.

It was a moment or two before Guy appeared, accompanied by a couple.

Hope would have liked to retreat to the drawing-room
but they spotted her before she could.

'Hope,' Guy called out, as if they were the best of
friends, 'I've brought some people home to see you.'

Reluctantly Hope stepped out of the shadows and
crossed the hall to the couple. The woman was in her
late thirties, slightly plump but attractive. The man was
tall and slim, perhaps Guy's age, but looked older because of his receding hairline.

Was she meant to know them? Hope wondered. They
did look slightly familiar.

'You don't remember us, do you?' The woman stepped
forward and beamed a smile at her. 'Well, that's un-
derstandable. I'm afraid I've gained a couple of stone
and Richard has lost most of his baby curls,' she admitted with a rich vein of amusement in her voice.

'Beth.' Hope found the woman's name as the voice
struck chords of recognition. 'Beth Castillon.'

'The very same,' Beth confirmed and, with a warmth
that took Hope by surprise, leaned forward to plant a

kiss on her cheek. 'And I have to say you don't look a day older,' she announced generously, after studying Hope's face.

Hope remembered the couple now. They lived just a couple of miles along the cliff-road from Heron's View. She had met them socially when out with Guy. Beth had also invited her over for coffee on a few occasions, and they had got on well, although Hope had been a little shy with the older woman.

'Don't you agree?' Beth prompted her husband.

'Not a day older,' Richard Castillon confirmed with a smile, and stepped forward to shake Hope's hand, 'although I seem to remember your hair was different.'

'It was long. Right down her back,' Guy answered for her, his tone abrupt.

Hope put a self-conscious hand to her cap of blonde hair. People told her the cropped style suited her, but Guy obviously didn't think so.

'Well, I wish I was slim enough to get away with your cut,' Beth rejoined, seeing Hope's face fall a little, and reassured her, 'It's so feminine, just right for your bone-structure.'

'Thanks.' Hope smiled shyly at the other woman's kindness and for a moment felt as she had twelve years ago, a child compared to Guy's confident friends. 'Have you...I mean, would you like some tea or something?' she added, feeling she should play hostess as Mrs Stevenson had the Sunday off.

'That would be lovely,' Beth accepted, with another beaming smile.

Guy looked surprised by the offer. Perhaps he imagined she had no social graces. Or did he think it a cheek, her playing mistress of the house?

Maybe not, for he surprised her in turn by saying, 'I'll come and help you.'

'Um...there's no need,' she dismissed, and quickly retreated to the back of the house where the kitchens were.

She was followed by Beth. 'I'll give you a hand,' she suggested, and proceeded to prove that she had more idea of where things were kept than Hope did. 'Sometimes I give dinner parties for Guy's more important clients,' she explained her knowledge of the kitchen. 'Mrs Stevenson is OK for meat and two veg, but she refuses to contemplate anything remotely exotic ... Is she giving you a hard time?'

'I—I've hardly met her,' Hope replied uncertainly.

'Well, if she tries, don't let her,' Beth suggested. 'She can be an awful cow to Guy's girlfriends.'

'I'm not a girlfriend,' Hope returned smartly.

'Well, no...' Beth looked at her askance for a moment. 'But she may not appreciate the fact, especially if Guy's as vague with her.'

'Vague? What do you mean?' Hope frowned quizzically.

'You know,' Beth replied easily. 'Guy never explains himself to other people. He told us you've returned for a while, but didn't give any reason. I'm burning with curiosity,' the older woman admitted frankly, 'but just tell me to mind my own business if you like.'

'Well...' For a moment Hope was tempted to explain about Jack's will, especially as Beth was so open and honest, but they were Guy's friends and if he didn't want them to know the truth it seemed underhand of her to betray him. 'It's a bit complicated. It might be better if you ask Guy.'

'Fair enough.' Beth didn't press her. 'Although that's like getting blood out of a stone, at times... Do you know, he never even told us you had a child—after you went away with Jack, I mean? I couldn't believe it when he introduced Maxine at the club, although I should have guessed. She's very like him, isn't she?' Beth smiled once more. 'Guy, I mean, not Jack.'

Hope stared at her for an instant, wondering if the smile hid something else—suspicion, speculation, knowledge? But perhaps it was just a smile, fondly acknowledging the likeness between Maxine and her 'uncle'.

Hope forced a smile back, but treated the question as rhetorical.

'She's a lovely girl, too,' Beth ran on, 'so pleasant and well-mannered.'

'*Maxine*?' Hope didn't recognise her daughter from the description.

Beth understood and laughed. 'It's the same with Natalie. People tell me what a kind, considerate, wonderful child she is. Not the Natalie I live with. She's a monster. Difficult, moody, resentful, arrogant, you name it,' she recounted, rolling her eyes.

Hope made a sympathetic sound. 'She can't be worse than Maxine.'

'Don't count on it,' Beth warned, 'although I suspect, from the whispering that went on soon after they met, that we may have a case of soul-mates.'

'How old is Natalie?' Hope was worried that Maxine might be older, and possibly a bad influence because of it.

'Thirteen,' Beth relayed.

Hope felt a measure of relief. 'Maxine's the same this month.'

'And they can't wait, can they?' Beth shook her head. 'Then they can officially act as teenagers and make our lives even more miserable.'

'Probably.' Hope smiled in agreement.

'You know, when she was little, the idea of boarding-school was absolutely repugnant to me,' Beth confided, 'but now it seems an increasingly attractive proposition.'

'Where does she go to school?' Hope had to find a school for Maxine to attend.

'Greenbrooke's, an independent near St Ives,' Beth relayed. 'It's academic without being too intense, and particularly well-rated for arts and music... Natalie professes to hate it, but went hysterical when I suggested sending her elsewhere,' Beth finished with a wry smile.

It sounded right for Maxine, who was academic enough, while having a definite talent for music, one that Hope could only foster in a limited way through piano lessons.

'Guy did suggest he might be interested for Maxine,' Beth added rather unwisely.

*He* might be interested? Hope echoed silently, wondering what right Guy Delacroix imagined he had over Maxine's education.

She shook her head and replied flatly, 'There'd be no point. We're only here for a few months.'

'Oh, I didn't realise.' Beth looked surprised. Guy had obviously given her a different impression. 'Well, as you say, if you're returning to London, it wouldn't be worth the hassle of getting her into Greenbrooke's... They don't so much vet the children as the parents. See if you have the right attitude,' Beth explained, laughing once more. 'Richard had to keep poking me in the ribs and telling me to be serious, and I had the distinct feeling I didn't really pass muster with the head mistress.'

'Well, I'd have no chance,' Hope confided, and the two women smiled conspiratorially at each other.

Then, as they finished making the tea, Beth suggested, 'Let's have it in here, and the men can come foraging for themselves.'

'Yes, fine.' Hope was quite happy to keep away from Guy and, sitting down at the kitchen table, the two women were soon chatting with ease. In fact, they were laughing, heads together, when their two girls appeared in search of food.

'What's so funny?' Natalie directed at her mother, but the tone could have been an echo of Maxine's.

'Nothing, darling,' Beth dismissed, but the two women caught each other's eye and started laughing again.

'Like schoolgirls,' Maxine tut-tutted to her friend, and the two looked pityingly at their respective mothers, before departing with Coke and crisps discovered in the pantry.

Guy and Richard appeared shortly thereafter to find the women still sitting at the table.

'Do you want tea?' Hope remembered she'd offered them some about half an hour ago.

'Don't worry about them.' Beth dismissed the men with a look. 'I'm sure boiling a kettle isn't totally beyond them.'

'My wife the feminist.' Richard pulled a face, but there was no force behind his words. 'I'd keep her away from Hope if I were you, Guy. It's infectious.'

'I'm sure Hope doesn't need any lessons from me about being independent,' Beth claimed, 'having brought up a daughter and pursued a career all on her own.'

Beth's tone was admiring. Guy's look was anything but.

'I doubt if Hope has lacked male company,' he commented flatly.

'I doubt it too.' Richard Castillon agreed, only he meant it as a compliment.

Hope's scowl was directed purely at Guy. He obviously imagined she'd had dozens of love-affairs.

Beth caught her expression and tried to smooth things over, saying, 'Typical men, they hate to think we can survive without them, whereas it's clearly the other way round.'

'Huh!' Richard laughed with mild scorn, before suggesting, 'In that case, you won't mind if Guy and I escape for a couple of hours. *The Mistress* needs a little attention.'

'No, you go if you like,' Beth shrugged. 'Just leave me the car so I can drive home.'

'Sure,' Richard nodded. 'We'll go in Guy's.'

'I'll drop him off later,' Guy confirmed, as if it were the most normal thing in the world.

Hope's mouth gaped open at the sheer casualness of the conversation. Richard had just admitted that he was going to visit his mistress and Beth hadn't batted an eyelid. It wasn't so much civilised as decadent.

It was Beth who caught her expression first and, realising, burst out laughing. Richard, realising too, joined in.

It was Guy who drily explained, '*The Mistress* is Richard's boat.'

'Oh.' Hope went red at her mistake.

But Beth hadn't taken offence. 'The name was my choice. Singularly appropriate, considering the time and money he lavishes on it. In fact, I suspect a real mistress would be cheaper.'

'I'll bear that in mind——' Richard smiled at his wife '—should we ever have to economise.'

'You do and I'll——' Beth began in warning.

'Rip my heart out—yes, I know,' Richard finished for her, and, dropping a kiss on her forehead, added, 'Come on, Guy, let's go sink a few beers and complain about women in general and my wife in particular.'

Beth pulled a face at her husband, saying to Guy, 'I trust you not to believe a word.'

'Don't worry, I will fence-sit as usual,' he promised, kissing the cheek presented to him by Beth, before murmuring to Hope, 'I'll see you later.'

Hope assumed it was said to support the illusion that she was staying at Heron's View by invitation rather than on sufferance, and she gave a nod in response.

When the men had departed, Beth said, 'I sometimes wonder if Richard really does complain to Guy and that's what puts him off marriage.'

'Is he, then?' Hope found herself asking, 'Off marriage, I mean.'

Beth shrugged, before revealing, 'Well, he seems to get cold feet at the remotest tinkling of wedding-bells. I shouldn't really gossip, of course, but...' The older woman hesitated, dying to confide in Hope, but unsure whether she should.

Hope said nothing. She wasn't sure if she wanted to hear about Guy's love-life.

It was her silence that tipped the balance in her favour. Beth took it for lack of interest and assumed that Hope's discretion could be guaranteed.

'Of course, I've been hugely relieved that he hasn't married some of the ladies he's dated,' Beth confided, 'but some have been really nice girls. He just seems to be unable to commit, poor Guy.'

'Poor girls, more like!' Hope commented with a vehemence that drew a surprised stare from Beth. 'I mean if he leads them on then dumps them.'

'Oh, no!' Beth protested in reply. 'Guy would never be so cruel. It's more a case of him detaching himself gradually, or them issuing ultimatums, or just giving up on him as a bad job. I don't know any girl who feels he's mistreated her.'

Beth was wrong. There was at least one. Hope felt he had mistreated *her*, making promises he hadn't kept.

Perhaps Beth read something in Hope's face as Hope kept rigidly silent. 'You know, Richard once thought that you and Guy...' the older woman ventured. 'Well, that if it hadn't been for Jack Guy might have...'

Receiving no encouragement from Hope, Beth trailed off.

This time Hope hid her feelings well, asking stonily, 'Might have what?'

'Um...nothing.' Beth pulled a face, dismissing the unspoken idea as she ran on, 'Still, there's always a chance that his current lady is Miss Right. Or Mrs Right, to be more exact.'

'Guy's dating a married woman?' Hope concluded in shocked tones, before she realised she was being hypocritical. Neither she nor Guy had been too bothered about her marriage during the brief weekend they'd spent as lovers.

'Divorced,' Beth corrected her. 'Liz Downing. Perhaps you remember her. Elizabeth Tremayne before she married.'

The name was vaguely familiar, but Hope shook her head. She wasn't sure if she wanted to hear more about Guy's current love.

But Beth was oblivious, adding, 'She was married to Paul Downing, the Conservative MP, for about ten years. She's about thirty-five. No kids. Quite nice woman, actually, and obviously keen on Guy. He could do worse, is my opinion, but he'd better get moving if they want children.'

Hope's heart sank a little. She didn't want to hear what a nice person Guy's current girlfriend was.

'I don't think Guy intends to have children.' She was repeating what Guy had told her when he'd promised to leave Heron's View to Maxine.

'Really?' Beth's eyes widened. 'Well, you do surprise me. I've always assumed Guy'll give up his bachelor status to have children. He's certainly been a marvellous godfather to Natalie. In fact, we've nominated him guardian if anything happens to us,' Beth confided with a deepening frown.

Hope realised that she'd made Beth anxious. If Guy didn't want children, was he likely to look after someone else's, should circumstances dictate?

'I probably got it wrong,' she added quickly, beginning to wonder if she had. Beth knew Guy better than she did. Perhaps it was to Hope that he had lied, in order to guarantee she would come down to Cornwall for the required six months.

Beth saw that Hope was worried now, and dismissed the issue with a shrug. 'Oh, well, who can tell with Guy? I've known him twenty years and I still can't tell what he's thinking much of the time,' she admitted, but in a fond tone, betraying her regard for him.

Hope didn't share it, but kept her feelings in check. She enjoyed the other woman's company and agreed to have lunch with her on the following Tuesday. Maxine was pleased too, for she and Natalie seemed to have become friends in a short period.

If it weren't for Guy, Hope reflected, life at Heron's View might be quite bearable.

# CHAPTER EIGHT

HER anger with him did not subside. She cooked spaghetti bolognese for tea, serving it up at the kitchen table just as he reappeared.

'Hi, Uncle Guy,' Maxine beamed, and got up to fetch an extra plate. She caught her mother's resentful look and said, 'There's enough, isn't there, Mum?'

'I suppose,' Hope admitted ungraciously, 'but maybe your uncle has other plans.'

'No, no other plans.' He smiled a little.

Hope's face remained stony as she ladled pasta on to his plate.

It wasn't much of a meal but he ate it all and said, 'Thanks, I enjoyed that.'

Hope acknowledged the comment with a sound that was more a grunt than anything else, and rose to clear the dishes.

Maxine remained at table with Guy, and suddenly brought up the matter of schools. Natalie had already sold her on the idea of Greenbrooke's. Hope wouldn't have minded if Maxine had consulted her first, but she hadn't. She was clearly asking Guy.

Guy was about to answer her when he caught sight of Hope's pursed lips and wisely decided to duck the question. 'Your mum and I have yet to discuss schools, Maxine, so perhaps you'd better leave it for now.'

Maxine opened her mouth, ready to argue as she always did, then thought better of it, observing Guy's shake of the head, the smallest of signals.

'All right.' She smiled at him, then addressed the dog quietly lying under the table. 'Come on, Rufus, walkies!'

The red setter was up and after her before Hope could wonder at the wisdom of an evening walk.

'She'll be OK.' Guy recognised her concern. 'It's still light and I've shown her the safe paths.'

Hope bit her lip, still worried. In London, Maxine wasn't allowed out on her own after six—because of the 'weirds', as Maxine herself put it. But was it fair to impose such a curfew in this remote part of Cornwall, where the chance of her coming to harm was minimal? Wouldn't it be good for her to taste some of the freedom and independence that country kids enjoyed?

'I'll go with her if you like,' he offered.

'No.' Hope felt that Maxine was already seeing too much of her uncle.

She ignored his questioning look and went back to stacking the dishwasher. She hoped he might take himself off to the living-room, but, though he stood up, it was to come round to her side of the table. 'What's wrong?' he finally asked, when she shut the machine and turned it on.

'Wrong?' Hope stiffened. 'What could possibly be wrong?'

'You tell me,' he suggested quietly.

Hope felt that if she started she would never stop. 'You mean besides the fact that my daughter consults you rather than me on her education?' She cited his latest sin.

He shook his head. 'I can't help that, and you were mad with me before that... Are you annoyed that I disappeared with Richard? I assumed you liked Beth.'

'I do,' she confirmed. 'I have no problem with Beth.'

'Just with me,' he concluded. 'So, let's hear it.'

'All right.' Hope's temper rose. 'Since you're asking. You told me that you weren't going to have children.'

He looked surprised by her line of attack. 'And?' he prompted, arching a brow.

Hope felt like hitting him. 'Beth's told me about Elizabeth Downing,' she said in accusing tones.

He remained perfectly calm. 'She's told you what exactly?'

'That there's a possibility you might marry her,' she stated bluntly.

There wasn't a flicker of reaction on his face to say whether it was true or false. She'd forgotten how unreadable he could be.

'So?' He lifted his shoulders in a shrug, then smiled a little mockingly. 'Should I assume you want an invitation to the wedding?'

'You——' Hope bit off the epithet that rose on her lips, but couldn't control her anger. 'Stuff your invitation! I want to know how it affects Maxine.'

'Sorry, you've lost me.' He was still so cool that Hope had to dig her nails into her palms to stop herself slapping him. 'Why should my marrying Elizabeth have any effect on Maxine?'

'If you have children,' Hope retorted at his intentional stupidity.

'Ah.' He pretended enlightenment. 'I thought I'd said. There will be no children.'

'How can you possibly say that?' she threw back at him. 'You marry this woman—any woman—and most are going to want children.'

'I'm well aware of that.' His voice hardened a little. 'Why do you think I haven't married? Did you imagine I was still pining for you?' He scorned the idea with a short laugh.

'Of course not!' she declared truthfully. 'I just don't understand...'

'Do you need me to spell it out for you?' He betrayed anger for the first time as the fingers on her arm tightened their grip.

'You don't like children?' Hope saw no other possibility, but answered for herself, 'I don't believe you. Not the way you are with Maxine.'

'You don't listen, do you?' he rasped back. 'I said there will be no children, not that I disliked them.'

'But why?' Hope searched his face for the truth.

He gave it brutally, saying, 'I believe the expression is firing blanks.'

'What?' It took Hope a moment to understand, then reject it with an equally blunt, 'You're lying!'

He laughed, but it was a harsh, unpleasant sound. 'Do you really imagine I'd lie about something like this?'

'I . . .' Hope stared at him in confusion, and, still shaking her head, muttered, 'How?'

'Mumps,' he answered shortly.

Hope knew what he meant. Mumps could make men sterile if caught outside childhood.

'When?' She matched his brevity.

'Ten years ago,' he informed her.

Hope continued to stare at him in horror. She didn't want to believe him, but she had a terrible feeling that it was true.

From her meetings over the years with his mother, she had known that Guy had never married. She had assumed he enjoyed his independence too much. But, like Beth Castillon, she had imagined he would marry one day, if only to continue the Delacroix line.

Now he was saying that there could be no children, whether he married or not, and the full implication of it hit Hope like a blow to the stomach. Perhaps he had longed for children; perhaps he still did. And here she was, able to give him one. She just needed to say the words. Admit. Confess. The mess of it.

She shut her eyes and he read her expression for pity. His fingers bit into her arm as he growled at her, 'Don't look like that! If I wanted pity, I wouldn't go to you.'

'Have you told——?' Hope began to ask him who knew.

He cut in, 'No one, and I expect things to remain that way. I am telling you so you know Heron's View will go to Maxine.'

'I'm—I'm so sorry.' Hope knew the words were inadequate.

His eyes raked her dismissively. 'For God's sake, it's not the end of the world. I accepted the fact years ago. There's a hell of a lot of people worse off than me. I may not be able to father children, but I can function normally,' he told her bluntly, then, at her continued silence, switched to mockery. 'Although perhaps you need convincing after last time.'

'Last time?' Hope echoed rather stupidly.

'Forgotten already?' He raised a reproachful brow. 'Well, let's see if I can jog your memory. June. Sunny afternoon. London. Your bed——'

'All right, I remember!' Hope cut across him before he could elaborate further.

'We were interrupted,' he ran on, smiling to himself, 'just as I was about to prove my manhood. So I can see you must have doubts now.'

'No, I—I . . .' Hope shook her head and took a step backwards. She came hard up against the sink. He placed an arm on either side of her, effectively hemming her in. She told herself not to panic. 'I—I don't.' She had no doubts. His virility always was and always would be overpowering.

'You're not scared of me?' He frowned as he lightly touched her cheek and she trembled.

She nodded, but it was a lie, and he knew it.

'I don't think so.' He placed a gentle hand on her shoulder and smiled slowly down at her.

The smile was disarming. She stared back at him. It was a mistake. She looked into those deep grey eyes of his and felt herself slipping away, slipping back, into the past and a time when she had been in love with this man.

'Please.' Her voice shook, she shook, as he lowered his head and touched his lips to her temple. She wanted him to stop. She needed him to stop. She didn't trust herself.

He understood, lifting his head away. She glanced down. He caught her chin and forced her to look at him again.

She was helpless. Her eyes betrayed her feelings. She wanted this man as she had no other.

He cupped her face with his hands, then slid his long fingers into her hair. She couldn't move, even if had she wished to. And she didn't.

His gaze rested on her face like a caress. Hope found his sudden switch to gentleness unbearable. She knew it couldn't be real, but it was hard to resist.

She felt his breath on her cheek. She knew he was about to kiss her. She just had to say no and mean it. She said nothing.

His mouth lightly covered hers in a kiss that seemed more loving than sexual. Her heart turned over. She slipped further from reality. She swayed a little and his hands went to her waist.

He drew her closer, and she lifted her hands to his chest, but she did not push him away. His kiss changed, his mouth hardening on hers until she opened her lips for him. She gasped as gentleness gave way to a rough sensuality. She felt the kick of her own desire and a moment's panic made her flinch away.

He lifted a hand to the back of her head and held her there, tasting her with his lips, his tongue, his teeth, forcing her to accept this terrible passion they had for each other, making her want and need, and give in to the sweet, bitter pleasure of loving him.

She was his, and he knew it. How could he not, when she clung to him, pressed her softness to his hard male body until he lifted her hips to his, betraying his own need of her? Then he started touching her, her arms, her back, her breasts, frustrated by her clothing, trying to push her blouse aside. She might have let him, might have lain with him right there and then, on the kitchen floor, if sanity hadn't returned.

For sanity came, for the second time, in the shape of her daughter—*their* daughter.

It was sheer luck that Maxine called out, 'Mum?' as she opened the back door into the scullery behind the kitchen. It gave Hope just enough time to break free and turn away, smooth down clothes, take a deep, unsteady breath, get herself ready to face a curious Maxine.

Maybe it was still obvious. Hope realised how it must look. She felt the heat in her cheeks that did nothing to hide her guilt and embarrassment.

Guy seemed unaffected, leaning back against the sink with his arms casually crossed, as if they'd been doing nothing more incriminating than discussing the weather. Angry at him, Hope snapped at Maxine, 'Yes?'

'I'm—I ... Sorry.' Maxine looked from one to the other, saw her mother's agitation, and assumed she'd just interrupted an argument. 'I put Rufus in his kennel for the night,' she muttered to Guy, before beating a hasty retreat.

Hope wanted to kick herself. Then she wanted to kick him, for not being in the least bit fazed.

'Never mind, third time lucky,' he said, catching her eye with his. His gaze was lazy, still desiring. He hadn't just been brought back to reality. He had never left it. He had no dreams of love, just the need for sex.

'There won't be a third time,' Hope claimed in a tight, angry voice.

He was unimpressed. 'Yes, there will,' he said in low, compelling tones. 'Just accept it. It's as inevitable as it was twelve years ago.'

Hope shook her head and put the space of the table between them, before she said, 'I won't let you use me like that again.'

His eyes lost their desire and became the cold grey they usually were. He laughed. A humourless sound. 'I think we have that the wrong way round, don't we?'

'I didn't use you!' Hope countered angrily.

'Oh, didn't you? Well, that's not how I remember things. One minute you're in my bed, promising to "come live with me and be my love",' he quoted softly, and continued harshly, 'the next you're driving off back to London with Jack.'

'That wasn't how it was,' Hope protested once more, but he wasn't going to be silenced.

'That's exactly how it was,' he rapped back. 'You slept with me to get back at Jack, then returned to him just long enough to dump him too... The only thing I can't figure is why you took so many years to get round to telling him about us.'

Hope felt both disbelief and anger. He had distorted everything. 'I slept with you because I was weak and lonely and stupid,' she admitted honestly, 'but there was no grand plan. Not like with you. You wanted me because I was Jack's, but you never really gave a damn about me.'

'How do you know what I felt?' He almost shouted the words at her.

'Because it was bloody obvious!' Hope threw back at him. 'When Jack turned up, you couldn't bale out fast enough. I tried talking to you but you didn't want to know.'

'What did you expect?' he growled. 'One moment you're agreeing to live with me, the next Jack appears and you're remembering your wedding-vows.'

'I wanted to do the right thing.' She recalled her confusion at the time.

'And that was to go back to hubby?' He gave a derisive laugh. 'So tell me, if that was true, how come you walked out on Jack within weeks?'

'I...' Hope had no defence unless she confessed about Maxine and that was impossible. She looked across the table between them, her eyes appealing for him to understand.

'All right, I'll tell you why,' he continued relentlessly. 'You slept with me to get even with Jack. Fair enough. More fool me for thinking it was anything else. You went back to Jack so you could dump him. That, I suppose, was fair enough too. He deserved it... Just stop making yourself out to be the victim. I didn't use you. You used me,' he accused in bitter tones.

'N-no, I—I didn't,' Hope stammered, incredulous at his version of events. Didn't he know how she'd felt? Their weekend together had been a dream, two days of complete happiness, after a year of misery. Jack's return had thrown her completely. She had longed for Guy to hold on to her, but his indifference had been chilling.

'You didn't care about me,' she said in a small voice as she recalled how hurt she'd been.

'Poor, pathetic little Hope!' His tone was scornful. 'It's so much easier to believe that, isn't it? So much nicer to have Jack and me both villains... Well, to hell with that. Jack might have treated you like dirt, but I didn't. I cared all right. God knows why, but I cared.'

Hope shook her head and kept shaking it. She didn't want to hear this. After all these years, she couldn't cope with it. She backed away from him, then turned to run.

He caught her at the kitchen door and dragged her round to face him. She cried at him, 'You're lying! You're lying!' and would have covered her ears, but he pulled her hands away.

'Why should I lie?' he rapped back at her. 'I told you then, I'm telling you now. I loved you. I loved you so much I would have turned my back on my brother, my mother, my home for you.'

'No!' Hope screamed at him. She wouldn't believe it, she couldn't.

She struck at him, over and over, until he finally released her, then she ran, out into the hall, and up the staircase, desperate to get away, to reach her room, to hide the terrible anguish she felt inside.

He had loved her, he'd said. But he couldn't have. It made things too unbearable.

She lay on her bed and forced herself to recall what had happened that last day all those years ago...

It had been the Monday. Guy had had a business meeting in Truro he couldn't miss. He'd promised to collect her in the afternoon, before his mother was due back. He had kissed her long and hard, as if he couldn't bear to leave her, and she had felt the same way. She had gone upstairs to pack. She had had no doubts then. She loved Guy. She was going to leave Heron's View and go and live with him in Truro.

Later, when she had heard a car screech to a halt on the gravel outside, she had assumed it was Guy coming back. She had rushed to the front door, only to find Jack on the doorstep. She had backed away from him, shaking her head, but he had caught her hand.

He had seen the distress on her face and concluded, 'You've had a letter too.'

'Letter?' For a moment Hope wasn't sure what he was talking about. She had forgotten about everything but herself and Guy.

'From Vicki,' Jack added, realising from her face that he wasn't welcome.

'Yes, of course.' Hope forced herself to concentrate, to react the way she should. 'Vicki says you had an affair,' she said, but it lacked any proper indignation.

Jack frowned, trying to guess her feelings. He'd expected fury, not disconnection.

'Not an affair.' He shook his head vehemently. 'You must believe that, *chérie*. I... It's true, I did... I was weak, I admit, but I care nothing for her.'

'Oh.' It took Hope a moment to sort out what he was saying. He had slept with Vicki but had no feelings for her. Was that meant to make things better?

She wondered what he was doing here, then recalled his first words. 'Did Vicki send you a letter as well?' she asked, still with that curious lack of emotion.

He nodded. 'She's angry because I refused to leave you. She knows it's you I love.' He gazed intently at her, as if to demonstrate his love.

Hope just felt sick and shocked. If she hadn't spent the weekend with Guy, she might have shouted at him, hit him, walked away from him. Now she didn't know what to do.

He saw her cases on the stairs. 'Please don't leave me. I've been a fool, I know, but you can't leave me. I love you. You're my wife.'

Hope stared at him in disbelief. 'You haven't been here in weeks—months, Jack,' she accused, 'so how can I be a wife to you?'

'I know, I know.' He threaded a distracted hand through his hair. 'I kept meaning to come but something always came up. But things will be different. I swear it. Just give me a chance,' he appealed with apparent sincerity.

But it barely touched Hope. She just wished she'd already escaped.

She listened helplessly as Jack promised her the moon if she went back to him. It meant nothing. She wasn't even sure she believed him.

Jack, who'd expected her either to hit him or fall into his arms, eventually noticed she was doing neither, and switched tactics.

' "Marriage should be forever", that's what you said,'
he reminded her quietly, 'and it's the way I want it too.
I've been weak. I admit it. I wasn't ready for the baby,
but losing it was worse. You were so unhappy and I
couldn't seem to do anything.'

Hope stared at him in surprise. She assumed he'd
stayed away out of indifference.

'But we just have to get on with our lives, Hope.' He
squeezed her hand gently. 'You and me. Learn to accept
there'll be no more babies and be everything to each
other.'

'No more babies'. The words echoed in her head. So
final and terrible. Words she had forgotten to say to Guy.
And if she did...

'I have to return to Paris,' Jack added, 'and I want—
need—you to go with me. Please.'

Hope didn't want to go. The idea put her stomach in
knots. But she suddenly saw her future: a failed marriage followed by a failed affair when Guy tired of her.
She thought of her father's life, moments of happiness
interspersing years of hard drinking and sad
relationships.

She shook her head at Jack, but he saw the uncer-
tainty in her eyes.

'All right, not Paris,' he conceded, 'but let me take
you to London, rent a flat for you there while you make
up your mind about our marriage. Just give it a try.'

Later Hope realised what a coward she'd been that
day. She had woken up next to Guy, full of courage,
more than willing to run off with him and damn the
consequences. But without Guy there to hold her hand,
give her some of his courage, she couldn't find any of
her own.

What Jack offered—her own place, time to decide,
some peace—suddenly seemed the easiest thing. It was
what she needed—the chance to sort out her life rather
than lurch from one crisis to another.

She gave an almost imperceptible nod, and Jack didn't waste any time. He kissed her on the cheek, before going to pick up her cases. 'We'll put these in my car and I'll leave a note for my mother.'

'I . . .' Hope watched him helplessly, already regretting that nod.

He carried her cases outside, but she didn't follow. She didn't want to go with him. She wanted to stay and be with Guy.

She heard a car crunch on the gravel outside and she went to the door. She saw Guy get out of his Jaguar and for a moment she felt the most enormous relief. He would take care of things. She just stopped herself from flying into his arms. She remembered in time that Guy wasn't only her lover; he was her husband's brother.

His eyes went from her to the cases Jack was loading, then back to her for a moment. She read the accusation in them and sent him an appealing look in return.

Jack was oblivious. 'I've come to get Hope,' he said to Guy, smiling now things had worked out his way.

'Really?' Guy's voice was cold as ice. 'And does Hope wish to be got?' He addressed his brother, but his eyes slid once more to Hope.

She shook her head. He didn't seem to notice as he looked back towards his brother.

'Of course, Hope's my wife.' Jack adopted a more defensive tone. 'I know I've neglected her lately, but things are going to be different now.'

A muscle worked at Guy's temple as he looked at his brother with hard disbelief, then at Hope, with derision, and he said just one word—'Congratulations'—before he walked right past her into the house.

Tears welled in Hope's eyes as she realised that he wasn't going to claim her.

Jack misunderstood. 'Don't let Guy upset you. It's me he's mad at. He thinks I've treated you badly.'

'I... It's not... I have to go and speak to him.' Hope didn't wait for a reply from Jack.

With a mounting sense of panic she searched for Guy, in room after room, before she realised he must have gone upstairs. She found him in his bedroom.

The door was ajar and he was standing by the window overlooking the sea. She stood in the doorway, unable to find the right words.

She eventually managed a soft, unsteady, 'Guy...'

He turned to face her. There was anger and contempt in his eyes, but no love.

Still she forced herself to go on. 'It's not—well, how it looks. Jack... He just appeared... He wants us to——'

'Don't worry!' he cut across her. 'I've got the picture.'

Hope shook her head. He didn't have the true picture. If he did, she would be in his arms and he would be saying, To hell with Jack, and they would be running away together. She loved this man.

Once more she tried to explain how she felt. 'I want to do the right thing, but I no longer know what that is. When I married Jack, I thought it would be for-ever——'

'Fine!' The word was shot at her, chilling and con-clusive. 'You don't have to quote your marriage-vows at me. I have no hold over you. You want to leave with Jack, then go.'

'Please listen...' Hope appealed, even as she won-dered if this hard-eyed stranger was the same man she had lain with just hours earlier.

'No, you listen,' he went on relentlessly. 'We had a brief affair—one of the briefest in history, I should im-agine. Let's not make a three-act opera out of it. Be-cause it was nothing. Just sex. Proximity. Curiosity.' He was denying any emotional involvement. 'So you can go trotting off back to hubby safe in the knowledge that I won't want to advertise our brief encounter either.'

Hope stared at him in shock, desperately seeking a sign that he didn't mean those brutal words, but his face was a dispassionate mask, stating that he did. She felt her own face was bare, betraying her feelings, the terrible aching love she had for him in her heart.

He must have seen something of it in her eyes, but it did not please him. 'Don't look at me like that!' he ordered harshly, and, when she went on staring at him, he crossed to where she stood at the door.

The next moment he had taken her into his arms and was kissing her, and her heart was leaping with the joy of it. But it was short-lived. He kissed her hard, then pushed her away from him, saying, 'And don't come back, all right?'

'I . . .' Hope saw no love in his eyes, just rage and contempt, and she felt as if her life was over. But pride sustained her; pride made her shake her head and say in a cold, dead voice, 'There's nothing to come back for,' before running from that room and him and her shattered dreams.

She went back to Jack inasmuch as she travelled in the same car with him, and let him rent her a flat in London for six months, and tried for a week or two to convince herself that their marriage could work. But she never loved him again, and could never bring herself to sleep with him.

Jack went away for some concert dates on the Continent and, by the time he returned, Hope knew she was pregnant by his brother Guy. She had not planned to pass Maxine off as Jack's. She hadn't imagined she could, as she and Jack hadn't been with each other for months. But it was one of those conversations that started out badly and got worse. Jack heard the word 'pregnant' and his horror was ill-disguised. He never gave her the chance to say, Don't worry, it's not yours. He assumed she was more pregnant than she was, and was too busy cursing the doctor who had said there would be no more babies, and making it plain that a child had no place in his life. Her options were limited—either motherhood on her own or a life with Jack minus baby.

It wasn't a hard choice. She said goodbye to Jack without a qualm, and he retaliated by stating that he would never pay a penny for the child. She told him then. The child wasn't his, so he didn't have to support it. He didn't believe her. Jack assumed it had been a thing said to hurt, and, when Hope wouldn't name an alternative father, that confirmed it.

By the time Maxine arrived two months early, Jack was no longer around, and, when he materialised years later, her birth date gave him no reason to doubt her parentage. Hope let things lie rather than have questions asked on who was the real father and felt no great guilt about it. Jack had lived up to his promise and had never supported her or Maxine in the intervening years.

It was odd, but she didn't feel so much bitterness towards Jack. She'd expected nothing better of him. It was Guy who had left her feeling devastated. For it was Guy she had loved, although she had spent a lifetime since then denying it.

Now he claimed that he had loved her, and she suddenly saw how wrong she might have been. She'd concluded that Guy had simply been interested in her because she was Jack's wife, and had taken his chance after Vicki's letter. But if that was so, if he'd been waiting to seduce her, why hadn't he told her about Vicki weeks earlier? He had known. He had even covered up for Jack.

She recalled what he'd said after the letter: he'd kept quiet for her sake, not Jack's. She'd been through so much—a difficult pregnancy, the stillbirth, her illness in New York. He had wanted to protect her from more pain. But could that have been true, when later he had caused her more grief than Jack ever could?

She thought of that last day at Heron's View and how things might have seemed to him. When he left in the

morning, it was with her 'I love you' whispered in his
ear and a promise to be ready when he returned. What
had he come back to? Her and Jack. Her, standing
around, compliant, while Jack put her cases in his car.
Too scared to declare her love, to trust in his. He had
read her silence as willingness to go with Jack and had
reacted accordingly. She'd assumed he hadn't loved her
because he had cast her off so easily, but had that contempt masked his own pain?

Hope shook her head. She couldn't start believing he
had loved her. It was too awful. To think that in less
than half an hour—from Jack's arrival to Guy's return—
the course of her life had been determined. And who
could she blame now? Not the Delacroixs, but herself,
for lacking the courage to hold on to Guy's love.

For a moment she pictured how things might have
been, living with Guy, having his baby, loving him more
as the years went on. No, it wouldn't have been like that.
She couldn't accept that. All those wasted years. No way
of getting them back. No way of getting him back. For
if he had loved her, the feelings were long dead.

She just wished her own were.

# CHAPTER NINE

'I CAN'T wait!' Maxine's blue eyes sparkled with excitement. 'Do you think I'll get to go water-skiing? Or scuba-diving? Or maybe——'

'As long as you don't ask,' Hope warned soberly as she packed her daughter's case.

'I won't. I never ask. Uncle Guy offers.' Maxine smiled at his generosity.

Hope sighed inwardly but said no more. They'd been at Heron's View almost a month, Maxine's birthday had come and gone, and she had long since given up trying to control Guy and Maxine's relationship. He treated his 'niece' with the same fond indulgence he'd once displayed to Hope, and Maxine, in turn, simply adored her 'uncle'.

It would have been easier for Hope if they'd disliked each other. The guilt would have been less. To see them so close didn't cause her jealousy as much as sadness, thinking of all the years they'd missed, been cheated of— arguably by her.

'You should come with us, Mum.' Maxine sensed her mother's dejection, if not the reason behind it.

Hope shook her head. 'You know I can't. I have meetings up in London, on top of that new jingle to do.'

Maxine pulled a face, but didn't argue. It was enough that she was going. Two and a half weeks cruising round the Mediterranean on a hired yacht with the Castillons and Guy.

Apparently Guy had spent other holidays with Beth and Richard Castillon, accompanied by various female friends. Hope had declined to be part of this year's crew.

149

Guy and she might have stopped fighting, but their politeness was almost as painful.

'You won't be taking anyone else's place,' Beth had assured her, when she'd refused the invitation. 'We thought Guy would be taking Elizabeth, but seemingly not. At least not on the boat. We may meet up with her on Crete.'

Hope, who already knew Guy wouldn't want her there, felt even less like going. She had met Elizabeth Downing twice. She was a thoroughly nice woman who happened to be in love with Guy. Hope would never dream of spoiling the other woman's chances, but she couldn't bear to watch them together either.

Suitcase packed, Hope carried it downstairs for Maxine. Guy was waiting in the hall.

'I've fed Rufus and put him in the kitchen,' he said to Hope. 'If you could walk him daily, I'd be grateful.'

'Of course.' Hope usually walked the red setter on days when Guy was working in Truro.

'And remember, if you have to go up to London, you can——'

'Call the kennels and they'll come and fetch him.'

Hope's expression was heavy with patience. He'd already told her all this.

'I'll just go and give Rufe a goodbye kiss,' Maxine announced, and disappeared towards the kitchen.

Hope's mouth quirked. She was beginning to feel that everyone was going to miss the dog more than her.

But when Maxine was out of earshot Guy said, 'You could still come with us. I could call the kennels now.'

'No, I can't.' Hope didn't believe he wanted her along, though he'd suggested it several times. She assumed it was for Maxine's sake.

'Well, you needn't worry,' he assured her. 'I'll look after Maxine.'

'Thanks.' Hope knew he would. In this, she trusted him. 'Sometimes she does silly things.'

'I've noticed,' he agreed drily. 'What one might call impetuous—like you used to be.'

Hope wasn't sure how to take the last comment. Was it critical of her now or then? Sometimes she herself felt a pale shadow of the girl she'd been when she'd first met Guy.

'We all grow up eventually,' she said, on the defensive.

'Yes,' he replied quietly, but he wasn't on the attack, as he added, 'You were very young—too young. Perhaps I should have waited.'

'For what?' Hope asked a little rashly.

'Till you'd got over Jack,' he replied bluntly, 'and were ready for me.

Hope stiffened and might have walked away had he not put a hand on her arm.

'We would never have worked.' She told him what she'd told herself many times over the last month. It was something she had to believe for her own sanity.

'Maybe not,' he agreed rather easily, 'but at least we would have had the chance to find out, to be free of each other.'

Hope's eyes widened. Did he feel as she did? Still emotionally trapped in a relationship that was over before it had really begun?

No, how could he? He had moved on, to other people, other loves, other dreams. It was she who was caught.

'We are free of each other,' she claimed out of pride. 'You have Elizabeth, remember?'

His eyes narrowed but he did not deny it, saying instead, 'And you have...?'

'None of your business,' she said, rather than make up another fictitious boyfriend.

But he knew the truth anyway, smiling as he said, 'No one...I've asked Maxine.'

'Don't you think that's underhand?' she retorted, but wasn't as angry as she should have been.

'Very,' he conceded, 'but all's fair in love and war. We just have to decide which this is.'

The word 'war' was on Hope's lips, as his flippancy sparked off the fight in her, but before she could say it Maxine appeared to announce the arrival of the Castillons.

He grimaced a little before saying drily, 'Why don't we both think about it while I'm away?'

'Think about what?' Maxine echoed.

'Future plans,' Guy answered, his eyes still on Hope.

Maxine grinned, putting her own meaning on the comment. Having succeeded in getting enrolled at Greenbrooke's, she had been working on Hope to consider moving to Cornwall on a permanent basis. She felt Guy might be on her side.

Hope scowled, not sure what he meant.

'Come on, Mum, Uncle Guy's just trying to be friends,' Maxine said, when she saw her expression. It wasn't the first time she had scolded her mother for being hostile to her uncle's friendly overtures.

Guy smiled as if to confirm his intentions. Hope forced a smile in return.

Maxine was pacified, and led the way outside to the Castillons vehicle, a roomy Renault Espace. They planned to drive to Portsmouth, leave their car at the port and take the ferry to Gibraltar, where their hired yacht would be waiting.

Beth greeted Hope with a warm smile and a last plea for her to come along. Hope made appropriate noises about work commitments before wishing both Castillons a great holiday.

Natalie signalled for Maxine to join her in the back row, but Maxine turned to her mother first and threw her arms round her, kissing her a little tearfully.

'Have a wonderful time.' Hope bit back her own tears, determined to send Maxine away light-hearted.

'I will.' Maxine's face brightened and she clambered into the back as Guy, having loaded the cases, held open the door.

'Look after her,' Hope appealed to Guy, suddenly conscious of losing her daughter, however briefly.

'I will,' he promised, before urging, 'Look after yourself, Hope.'

Unsure how to respond, Hope remained silent, then gasped with surprise at his next move. He gathered her close for a moment, kissing her hard, if briefly, on the mouth, before climbing into the Espace.

Hope wasn't given a chance to react. She was left with the imprint of his mouth on hers and her heart thudding painfully against her ribs. Maxine waved wildly as the car moved away and, waving back, Hope prayed she had not seen Guy kiss her. Maxine was old enough to believe in romance but too young to distinguish love from sex.

Fortunately Hope knew the difference. She understood what Guy had been saying. When their brief affair had ended, the love had died too, but not the sexual attraction. Guy might not like her much, but he still wanted her, and Hope would have to be naïve not to know that. She just wished she didn't feel the same way—and more, because she wasn't so good at separating sex and love.

Guy might make love to her a few times, then be free to move on. She would be the one left nursing a broken heart.

Hope couldn't go through that again. She thought of leaving before they returned, but she couldn't—not without cheating Maxine of her inheritance. Yet what alternative was there?

She found an answer later that day, in the shape of Elizabeth Downing. She arrived at the house in the afternoon, having misunderstood when Guy was leaving. Hope invited her in for coffee out of politeness, and was a little surprised when she accepted.

'I'm sorry to have missed him,' she said of Guy, when they were seated in the kitchen. 'Still, I'll be seeing him in a few days.'

'Yes, you're going out to Crete, aren't you?' Hope repeated what she'd heard from Beth.

The other woman nodded. 'I was going to sail with them, but, to be honest, I'm not much of a sailor. I go to the yacht club more for...recreational reasons.'

Hope guessed she meant Guy, and felt a pang of jealousy, hastily suppressed.

'Do you sail?' Elizabeth asked her.

'I did,' Hope admitted, 'but that was years ago.'

'When you first lived at Heron's View?' Elizabeth pursued.

'Yes,' Hope confirmed simply.

She assumed they were making casual conversation until Elizabeth ran on, 'In fact, didn't Guy teach you to sail?'

'Yes.' Hope frowned a little. 'How did you know that?'

'I...can't remember.' Elizabeth looked uncomfortable for a moment. 'Probably from Beth. She mentioned that Guy had looked after you when your husband was abroad.'

'Yes, I suppose he did.' Hope wondered how the other woman would react if she told her just how well Guy had looked after her, but she couldn't bring herself to do it. Her war, if it was one, was with Guy.

'That's Guy, of course.' Elizabeth smiled at the thought. 'He was a tower of strength to me when...well, when my husband left me.'

'Really?' Hope's smile was strictly polite as she wondered if this indicated some curious bent in Guy's personality—a compulsion to help abandoned wives. Had he also initiated an affair with this woman, while comforting her?

Hope's lack of comment prompted Elizabeth to confess in a rush, 'My husband left me for his researcher. She was five months pregnant. Par for the course among MPs, I believe.' She made a slight face.

'I'm sorry,' Hope said with genuine sympathy.

'I'm not,' Elizabeth rejoined. 'Not now, anyway. Of course I was upset at the time... He'd always maintained he didn't want children,' she added, more to herself than to Hope.

But Hope asked in reply, 'Did you?'

'Want children?' Elizabeth gave the matter a moment's consideration. 'Well, if Paul had said...I suppose I would have.'

It was hardly a positive response. It seemed Elizabeth Downing was dutiful wife rather than earth-mother material. Always dressed immaculately, in creams and pinks and lilacs, her blonde hair beautifully coiffured, she might be the sort of woman who regarded children as primarily messy beings. Had she had her own, no doubt a nanny would have been an absolute must. She was also no dog-lover, having wrinkled her nose at Rufus's tail-wagging advances, until Hope had felt obliged to call the dog to her side.

'Guy seems to like children,' Elizabeth resumed at Hope's silence. 'He's obviously fond of your daughter.'

'Yes.' Hope's guilty feelings stirred once more. If only Guy could have fathered other children...

Or had a happy marriage? The thought came to Hope as her eyes rested on Elizabeth Downing. Beautiful. Chic. Well-mannered. Undemanding. Too perfect for words.

Jealousy warred with a better impulse, and the better impulse won.

'But I don't think he'd want any of his own,' Hope announced on a purposeful note.

'Really?' Elizabeth's expression was eager, waiting for more.

Hope finally understood why she'd come. Not to see Guy, who she probably knew had already left, but to discover Hope's place in the scheme of things. Having discovered she was just a sister-in-law, she was now looking for pointers.

'Are you sure?' she prompted.

Hope nodded. 'It may be the reason he's never married. Most women want children, don't they?'

'Do they?' Elizabeth caught on fast. 'I can't say I've ever had a strong urge in that direction.'

Hope suspected Elizabeth Downing had never had a strong urge in any direction. She was beginning to regret giving her any assistance in winning Guy. Didn't he deserve better?

But, having started, Hope felt she needed to finish.

'Perhaps you should tell Guy that, let him know he's not on his own in that respect.'

A fairly heavy hint—it was up to Elizabeth if she wanted to take it, and to Guy, if he wanted to respond.

Hope resolved to interfere no further and switched to making idle conversation. Elizabeth took her leave soon afterwards, and Hope did her best to forget the interlude. If she dwelled too long on Guy and the other woman—any other woman—she felt sick at heart.

It was ten days later when she was forced to recall her encounter with Elizabeth Downing.

It had been a lonely ten days, apart from the silent companionship offered by Rufus, in Guy's absence constantly padding at her side. Maxine had telephoned a few times. She'd been full of the holiday, the Castillons, the sailing, the diving, the water-skiing, loving it all. And clearly loving Guy, as his name prefixed so many sentences. Guy did such and such. Guy said this. Guy thought that. As the closeness of father and daughter grew, so did Hope's guilt.

And then there was her jealousy. Not of their relationship but of Guy and Elizabeth Downing's. According to Maxine, Elizabeth had met them in Crete, as planned, and was talking of sailing back with them to Gibraltar. The news was like a stone in Hope's heart. Had she really believed it would make her feel better, Guy getting together with this other woman?

It was at this stage of their itinerary that Hope had her first and last conversation with Guy. Maxine was just finishing relaying the day's events, when she added, 'Uncle Guy wants a word. Bye, Mum. Take care.'

'You too,' Hope said before Maxine disappeared off the line.

Then Guy came on. There were no hellos, no how-are-yous. Just straight to the point. 'What have you been saying to Liz?'

'Saying?' Hope stalled for time, before deciding to feign innocence. 'About what?'

'You know damn well what about!' was barked back in her ear.

'I haven't told her about us,' Hope informed him, 'if that's what you mean.'

'I realised that,' he returned heavily. 'I want to know exactly what you said on the subject of children, in particular with regard to my ability to have them or not.'

'I... Nothing!' Hope was genuinely indignant. 'I wouldn't break a confidence like that.'

'Oh, really?' Disbelief made his voice as hard as granite. 'So tell me, why has Liz a positive compulsion to tell me she has no desire to reproduce? Once yesterday, twice today. With increasingly embarrassing obviousness... I repeat, what have you said?'

'Nothing... Well, nothing much.' Hope became defensive and bent the truth slightly. 'We were simply having a conversation about children and she said she'd never felt any pressing need for a family. I just happened to mention you hadn't either.'

'I see.' His voice was now ice. 'And how do you know what I feel? Have you ever asked?'

'I—I . . . No . . . but . . .' Hope couldn't explain her real motivation. It seemed ridiculous now. 'I was just trying to help,' she added feebly.

'*Help*!' he exploded at the other end of the line. 'Help who? Liz? Me? Or yourself?'

The latter made Hope protest, 'It hardly affects me, if you and Elizabeth Downing get married.'

'So that was the grand plan. Liz tells me she doesn't want children and, on the strength of that, I'm meant to propose,' he concluded with biting sarcasm.

'Not exactly,' Hope denied weakly.

'Well, what exactly?' he demanded in response.

'I . . .' Hope opened her mouth, then shut it. She seemed to be digging a bigger and bigger hole for herself. Perhaps now was the time to jump in it.

'Do you think I'm that desperate?' he rapped back at her silence. 'Is that it? You think I need your match-making efforts?'

'No, of course not.' She tried to pacify him but he wasn't listening.

'Or are you stupid enough to imagine I'd accept Liz Downing in your place?' he growled into the phone.

His bluntness threw Hope for a moment. 'I—I don't— don't know what you mean,' she eventually stammered out.

'Don't you?' His tone turned low and mocking. 'Well, let me spell it out for you. I could make love to Liz Downing morning, noon and night for the next week, but it won't change things between you and me. I want you, Hope Gardener, and you want me, and the moment I get back I'm going to have you,' he announced in cool, precise tones.

He couldn't have made his desire more explicit, and for an instant Hope's own senses reeled with the sheer overpowering sexuality of the man. He was a thousand miles away, but she remembered perfectly his touch, smell and taste from the last time she'd been in his arms.

She struggled for sanity and found it in his words. He would 'make love' to Liz Downing. He would 'have' her. A sex object. Desired but not loved. Not worth his respect.

Having worked herself into anger, she spat back down the phone, 'Tough! I won't be here.'

'What do you mean?'

'What I said. I'm leaving.'

It stopped him in his tracks for a moment. 'You can't,' he eventually responded. 'What about Maxine?'

'You can put Maxine on a train to London,' she declared wildly. 'I'll collect her at the other end.'

'Like hell!' he dismissed. 'Maxine starts at Greenbrooke's in less than two weeks. Remember?'

Hope wasn't likely to have forgotten. Emotional blackmail had been applied until she had finally agreed to Maxine's trying for a place at the school. A combination of Guy's persuasiveness and Maxine's marked musical ability had won over the headmistress. No mention had been made of her stay being limited to a term. Guy had paid the fees, arguing that it was his responsibility for having disrupted her education. Hope had accepted reluctantly.

'Not any more,' she retorted now, 'but don't worry. You'll be able to get a refund, I'm sure.'

'You can't do that,' he threw back. 'Maxine has her heart set on going there. You can't use her to get back at me.'

'All right! Fine! Great!' Hope over-reacted in temper. 'Maxine can stay in Cornwall if she likes. Why not? Stay with good old Uncle Guy. I'm sure she'll be delighted.'

'Hope!' Guy shouted down the line at her. 'Stop being melodramatic! Maxine's not going to stay anywhere without you. She's missing you enough as it is.'

'Oh, yes?' Hope had detected no sign of this from Maxine's phone calls. 'I'm returning to London as soon as possible. It's Maxine's choice what she prefers to do. Unless, of course, you don't want her.'

'Hope,' he repeated in a more calming tone, 'I don't know why you're saying all this. You're not being rational. Naturally I'd look after Maxine, should anything ever happen to you. But forcing her to choose, that's...' He trailed off, searching for the appropriate word. He didn't find it, but another thought occurred to him. 'That's what you did with her and her father, isn't it?'

'Her father?' Hope echoed blankly, then just as stupidly asked, 'You mean Jack?'

'Of course I mean Jack,' he said with impatience. 'Who else would I mean?'

'Nobody!' she snapped, furious at her own foolishness, and decided it was time to stop this conversation. It was already well out of hand.

She did so by the simple expedient of hanging up on him. She was still standing by the phone when it rang again. She picked it up automatically.

'Look, Hope,' Guy's voice came through the ear-piece once more, 'don't do anything silly until I get back. We have to talk——'

'I don't want to,' Hope cut across him, and muttered a final, 'Goodbye, Guy,' before replacing the receiver.

It didn't ring again and Hope was left in peace for the rest of the night.

Only it could hardly be called such, as panicked thoughts flew round her head. She had to leave, to run away from Guy Delacroix and her own weakness. She had to go before need and desire became confused with love, and led her to his bed once more. She had to escape before guilt tortured her into confession about Maxine. If that happened, she really would lose her daughter.

When daylight came, she had changed her plans slightly. She would have to wait in Cornwall for Maxine's return, then tell her they had to move back to London for work reasons. It sounded simple enough, but Hope knew it would be hard. She would probably have to drag Maxine home, kicking and screaming.

But what other choice did she have? Stay for Maxine, and lose her will, her pride, herself, to Guy Delacroix? She couldn't go down that road again.

She'd already arranged to go to London for a meeting. After a man from the kennels had fetched a reluctant Rufus, she went on an early train and stayed overnight at her house, getting it ready for re-occupation. In eight days, she calculated, Maxine would be on the ferry home from Gibraltar to Portsmouth. In nine, they would be on the train back to London. Hope refused to contemplate any other outcome.

But, of course, she hadn't reckoned with Guy. He turned up, ready for a fight, but not in eight days. He was waiting at Heron's View when she returned from her meeting in London.

She realised someone was inside the house the moment she entered. Instead of the letters being on the mat, they'd been placed on the hall-stand. Her first thought was of burglars, and she jumped a little when she heard footsteps.

Guy appeared from the kitchen. Hope felt relieved, then tense again. On second thoughts, she might have preferred burglars.

'What are you doing here?' she demanded, then, in panic, asked, 'Has something happened to Maxine?'

'No, she's fine,' he told her quickly. 'Beth and Richard are looking after her until I return.'

'To Crete?' Hope struggled to catch up with events.

He shook his head. 'They'll have moved on to Malta by then. We'll be home a couple of days later, but

Richard and Beth don't mind. I've explained things to them.'

'Oh.' Hope wished he'd explain things to her. Why was he here?

'I thought you'd already left,' he went on in the same level tones, 'but then I checked your room and saw most of your clothes were still there. I assume Rufus is at the kennels?'

Hope nodded, then began indignantly, 'I... You have no right——'

'Haven't I?' he cut across her. 'If you're dumping Maxine on me, I need to know. Make plans.'

'Of course I'm not!' she denied angrily. 'Maxine's coming back to London with me.'

He shook his head again. 'She says not.'

'Maxine says...?' she echoed, not following.

His brow creased. 'Unfortunately she overheard the tail-end of our telephone conversation. She wants to stay in Cornwall.'

'You've talked her round!' Hope accused.

'Not guilty,' he countered. 'You managed that all by yourself. Naturally she's angry and upset that you're prepared to take off without her.'

'That's not true.' Hope couldn't believe the way things had been twisted. 'What I said I said in temper. Do you really believe I'd abandon her?' she demanded furiously.

He remained maddeningly calm. 'No, I don't. Which is why I'm here—to take you back over with me so you can talk to her.'

'You're joking!' exclaimed Hope, then saw from his face that he wasn't. 'This is ridiculous. Why didn't you bring Maxine back home with you?'

'Apart from the fact that she refused point-blank to come, you mean?' he enquired drily. 'Of course, I could have tied her up and bundled her on the plane, but I didn't really fancy being arrested for kidnapping...

Besides which, you've already spoiled her holiday enough, so it's up to you to do the running.'

Hope breathed very deeply to keep her temper at the injustice of it. If she'd said some wild things over the telephone, it was because he'd made her. The whole thing was his fault, not hers.

'We can fly to Malta,' he went on, as if it was a foregone conclusion. 'I'll book a couple of singles, then it's your choice if you want to sail back with us or fly when you've made your peace with Maxine.'

Hope frowned. 'Is she very upset?'

'She was,' he relayed, 'but I've managed to calm her down.'

Hope wondered what he'd said. But he didn't volunteer any further information.

'I'll come to Malta,' she conceded, 'but I won't agree to staying in Cornwall. I can't.'

'Because of me?' He caught her eye for a moment.

Hope made the mistake of returning his stare. She felt his attraction like a physical blow, and looked away before she could betray herself.

'What if I promise not to touch you again?' he added on a harsh note.

Hope's lips tightened at his bluntness and her eyes reflected her distrust. She didn't have to speak for him to understand.

He gave a short, humourless laugh. 'You're right. It's a promise I won't be able to keep... But you'll at least come to Malta?'

Hope nodded. She felt she had to straighten things out with Maxine. She should have talked to her before announcing any decisions.

'And sail back with us?' he added as he crossed the hall to the telephone.

Hope wondered if he could be serious. 'Don't you think we'd be a little overcrowded—five adults and two children on a six-berth boat?'

'Five?' He lifted a brow. 'You, me, Beth and Richard. That's four.'

'And Elizabeth,' Hope reminded him, although it must hardly have been necessary.

His face tightened. 'Elizabeth is staying on Crete.'

'Oh. What happened?' Hope asked before she could stop herself.

'Do you want a blow-by-blow account——' he folded his arms and tilted his head at a sarcastic angle '—or will a summary do?'

Hope got the point and didn't blame him. 'Sorry, it's none of my business.'

'No, it's not,' he agreed, 'but that didn't seem to stop you... And, thanks to you, my relationship with Elizabeth has reached its inevitable conclusion.'

Hope's stomach went into a tight, hard ball. They were getting married. Thanks to her, he had proposed to nice, safe, suitable Elizabeth Downing and she had accepted.

'I—I...' Hope swallowed hard as she searched for the right response. 'That's... Con—congratulations,' she finally managed with a leaden heart.

'*Congratulations*?' he echoed, as if it was wildly inappropriate. 'You think——' he seemed angry for a moment, but then suddenly switched to a derisive sort of humour '—that Elizabeth and I make a good couple?'

'I—I d-don't know.' Hope felt sick at heart. 'I suppose. You have a lot in common.'

'Really?' He lifted a brow. 'What exactly?'

'I...' Hope wondered why he was doing this. Did he know how much she was hurting? Did he want to hurt her more?

She gave him a dismissive glance, before muttering, 'I'm going upstairs.'

'Yes, you do that,' he said to her retreating back, 'and I'll stay down here, counting my blessings.'

He followed her to the foot of the stairs as she quickly continued up them. She looked down for a last time to find him watching her, his face expressionless.

She went to her room and shut her door. She didn't lock it, although there was a key. He might be acting strangely, but Hope didn't fear Guy. Not in that way.

For Hope had finally faced the truth. It wasn't Guy that scared her. It was her own weak will.

# CHAPTER TEN

HOPE remained upstairs, skipping dinner. Fortunately she'd had a large restaurant lunch with an advertising executive and could survive till morning. She didn't want to encounter Guy again until she'd got over his marriage announcement. Would she have advised Elizabeth, had she known how devastated she would feel?

She still felt bereft when he knocked on her bedroom door at ten.

'Hope,' he called out when she didn't answer.

She still kept quiet. Already changed into her night-clothes, she wanted no more confrontations. She just wanted to crawl into bed and pull the covers over her head.

He knocked again, saying, 'Maxine's on the telephone. She wants to speak to you.'

It was a request Hope could hardly ignore.

'OK,' she called back, and quickly slipped into her dressing-gown before opening the door.

He stood on the threshold, with the mobile phone in his hand.

'Here.' He handed her the phone. 'I'll have it back when you've finished. I'm waiting for a call.'

She nodded. 'All right, thanks.'

He turned on his heel and she shut her door again, before going to sit on the bed. She took a breath, knowing the conversation was going to be difficult.

How difficult, she didn't quite realise. It began pleasantly enough, with them both anxious to make up. Then Maxine, intent on going to Greenbrooke's with Natalie, moved from persuasive to wheedling to downright bloody-minded when Hope failed to give way. Hope, realising that they were on the point of no return, eventually concluded the conversation with the suggestion that they talk more when she arrived in Malta. Maxine rang off with a last cry of, 'I don't want to go back to London, ever!'

Hope suspected she was going to fare no better in a face-to-face conversation. The problem was that she wasn't unsympathetic to Maxine's cause. She should have known that her daughter would either love or hate Cornwall, and, loving it, wouldn't want to leave. She should have realised that Guy might automatically become a father-figure to her. She should have remembered that, having set her mind on something, Maxine was almost impossible to shift. In short, she should never have come to Heron's View.

She felt angry with herself, then turned it on Guy when he appeared for his telephone. She answered his first knock and shoved it into his hand. 'Here!'

She would have shut the door but he stepped forward. 'Should I take it the conversation didn't go well?' he read from her expression.

'What do you expect? You and Natalie did too good a selling job on Greenbrooke's,' she accused, glaring at him.

'Come on, Hope,' he responded, 'you went round the place yourself. You saw the facilities. You heard the headmistress. Maxine's musical talents are going to be fostered there as they never were in her old school. Is it any surprise she's keen?'

Hope was unable to deny it. She shook her head and, deciding an argument with him on top of the one she'd just had with Maxine was too much for one night, turned away.

He remained in the doorway. She crossed her room to look out of the window. She hoped he would get the message and leave. The door shut, but with him on the wrong side of it.

'I don't understand you, Hope,' he continued in reasonable tones. 'I know you love Maxine. Don't you want the best for her?'

'Of course I do!' She rounded on him, angry that he might suggest otherwise. 'But that's not the point. She should never have been shown the place. I shouldn't have let you. Even if I stay the necessary six months, what then? Maxine's still going to have to go back to her old school, only now more resentful and unhappy because she's had a taste of something else.'

'She doesn't *have* to go back,' Guy countered.

'What do you mean?'

'What I said. Maxine could stay at Greenbrooke's. You could stay here.'

Hope looked at him in confusion. 'You mean permanently?'

'Yes,' he nodded. 'It'll be half your house, remember?'

'B-but...' Hope wondered if he could possibly be serious. 'It'll be over five years before Maxine completes her school education. You can't want us living here all that time.'

'What *I* want—when has that ever been relevant to you?' His mouth twisted slightly. 'It's certainly not the issue in this case. If you choose, you can remain at Heron's View for the rest of your life and there's not a thing I can do about it. Check with the solicitors if you don't believe me.'

Hope stared at him, open-mouthed. Why was he saying all this? Wasn't he counting the days till they left?

'Look, forget you and me, and our argument, for a moment,' he resumed. 'We've messed up our lives. What about Maxine? Don't you think she deserves a better chance?'

'That's not fair,' Hope accused as he worked on her guilt. 'Even if we did stay, I could never afford Greenbrooke's on a long-term basis.'

'I could,' he pointed out, but wasn't surprised at her immediate reaction.

'She's my child!' she exclaimed, dismissing the idea out of hand. 'I've always paid for her upbringing, and I always will.'

'All right,' he conceded, ready with another argument. 'There's your house in Putney. You could sell it and invest the proceeds for her school fees, or you could rent it out. The high rental rates in London should more than cover her fees.'

'That's not...' Hope was about to say 'feasible', but stopped herself as she realised it was. Quite feasible. She switched to saying, 'You can't want us here. You don't even like me.'

'You're right. Liking doesn't approach my feelings for you,' he admitted without excuse, 'but I do like Maxine. She's a bright, charming, lovely girl of whom you can be justly proud, but I think the next few years are the most important in her life. Kids can go so easily off the rails, especially in cities.'

He was saying nothing that Hope hadn't thought herself. As a teenager Maxine was going to need some careful handling. Greenbrooke's, with extra-curricular activities every night of the week, aimed to keep its pupils busy and, hence, out of trouble.

'All right.' She sighed in resignation.

'All right what?'

'She can go to Greenbrooke's—permanently, if she likes it. I'll do as you suggest and sell my house.'

'And stay here?'

Hope shook her head. 'No, there's only one solution. I'll rent a bed-sit in London. It means me losing my daughter for a large part of the year, but Maxine comes first. She can come home to me in the holidays, and stay with you during term-time...if that's acceptable to you?' she concluded.

'Of course,' he said immediately, 'but I think you should give yourself some time to consider. Wouldn't you be better off staying here? We can convert part of the house into a flat, if that's what you'd prefer.'

Hope frowned. She'd never really understood Guy in the past, and still didn't now.

'Thanks, but it wouldn't work,' she dismissed. 'Not with your getting married... In fact, your fiancée may not appreciate Maxine being in residence either.'

He sighed heavily. 'Elizabeth, you mean?'

'Unless you have two fiancées,' Hope flipped back.

'Elizabeth will have to accept it,' he replied arrogantly.

'You'd put Maxine first?' she challenged in disbelief.

'Of course. She's my flesh and blood, after all...isn't she?' he said meaningfully.

Hope saw anger in his eyes and misunderstood the reason. 'You know...'

'I know,' he repeated her shocked whisper. 'Know what?'

Hope went red, then pale, realising her mistake. 'Nothing. I thought... Nothing.' She recovered herself badly.

She was too late, as he pursued, 'What is there to know, Hope? Are you trying to say she *isn't* my flesh and blood? That she isn't Jack's?'

'I...' Hope didn't know which way to jump to avoid the hole that had opened up in front of her.

But he was already racing on. 'No, that's impossible. She looks too much like my father, too much like me.'

Hope felt her cheeks go a revealing red once more. She couldn't do anything to stop it. He stared hard at her.

'Too much like me.' He repeated the words and watched her reaction.

Hope tried to remain calm and expressionless, but she felt as if she had a neon sign on her forehead, flashing the word 'guilty' in big letters. He started closing the space between them, and Hope reeled away to face the window and the night outside.

But he didn't need to see her face or read her eyes. He jumped to the right conclusion, even as he said in harsh disbelief, 'No, she can't be. I worked it out. Years ago, when my mother told me there'd been a child, I worked it out... Tell me she can't be, Hope.'

Hope sensed him standing behind her but she didn't turn. Her throat was choked with a denial; she just couldn't get it out. Another lie. What would it matter? It sounded as if he wanted her to tell it. But she couldn't get it out.

Hard hands grabbed her arms and forced her round. She risked looking at him and saw shock and fury contorting his features. His fingers bit into her arms as he demanded, 'She was premature—like Samuel?'

Hope still could have denied it, but she was too surprised to answer. He had remembered her first baby's name. The boy who had died. She had thought only she carried that memory. Jack had certainly long forgotten.

She nodded. She gave him his child. She knew now that he would want her, would always have wanted her. If he was angry, it was at what she'd cheated him out of.

'God,' he breathed in an unsteady voice. 'You bitch... How could you?'

'I—I didn't know,' she stammered out.

'Which of us was the father?' he sneered in reply.

She shook her head. 'I always knew that. I didn't know if you'd want a child.'

'So you kept it to yourself,' he concluded at her weak responses, 'and passed it off as Jack's.'

'I told him the truth,' she claimed in her defence. 'I told him it wasn't his baby I was expecting. But he didn't believe me. Not until last year, when he guessed.'

'He knew I was the father?' Guy demanded, temper rapidly replacing initial shock.

Hope nodded, then flinched at the look on his face.

'I could kill you both,' he threatened hoarsely.

'You'll have to settle for killing me,' Hope replied in a quiet voice.

She wasn't joking. He wasn't either. The hands that held her were already bruising the soft flesh of her arms.

'I'll settle for something else,' he growled down at her, his face a mask of rage.

Hope understood. 'If that's what you want.' She felt she deserved some kind of punishment.

'You bitch!' he cursed her again even as he dragged her body to his. 'Don't go all compliant on me. I want you to kick and slap and scream. I want you to hurt the way I'm hurting. Do you understand?' he snarled without giving her the chance to answer.

His mouth was covering hers, teeth clashing, biting, cutting her lip. Not love but hate as he pushed her blindly backwards until she fell on the bed. No caresses but a curse as he lay down beside her and started to pull away her nightclothes, his hands hard and urgent and hurting.

Hope didn't kick or bite or slap. She didn't cry out. She just cried. Silent tears streamed down her face to her mouth, mingling with blood and saliva, as he continued to kiss her with hate in his heart.

Guy tasted the bitter salt of her tears and raised his head. He looked down at her stricken face and said in a low, harsh voice, 'Dammit, don't cry on me!'

'I—I can't h-help it,' she choked back, her eyes limpid with tears.

'Oh, for God's sake!' He shifted his weight off her and sat up on the bed.

Hope watched as he pushed a furious hand through his hair. She lay where she was, wondering why everything had to be like this. She remembered how it had been all those years ago, how she had felt such love for this man, and knew she felt the same now. When he turned to look at her again, she didn't try to hide her feelings for him.

But he misunderstood, mistaking passivity for fear. 'Don't look like that. I won't hurt you. Not that way.'

'I know,' Hope said softly even as she unconsciously fingered her lip where it was split.

His eyes were drawn to the movement. He reached out his hand and took hers away from her mouth. He winced on seeing the damage he'd done. 'It seems I already have.'

'It doesn't matter.' Hope felt his anger justified. She had stolen his daughter's childhood from him, without really appreciating the fact.

Yet his anger seemed to have subsided, as he muttered, 'I'll get you something,' and shifted off the bed to cross to the basin in the corner of the room. He ran the tap for a moment, then came back with a dampened facecloth. Hope sat up on the bed and he gently pressed it to her mouth. 'Any good?'

Hope nodded absently. The real pain was in her heart, as she realised what she'd lost. The love of this strong, honourable man. Why hadn't she fought for him? Why hadn't she told Jack that day he'd come back to claim her? Just told him straight: It's your brother I love. But she had lacked the courage and Guy, believing she'd made her choice, had walked away.

She sensed he was about to leave her again, and this time found the courage. She put her hand on his arm and said, 'Please stay.'

'Stay?' His face reflected doubt. 'You mean...?'

'Yes.' Hope didn't make him say the words. She tilted her head to his, and, when he failed to understand the love in her eyes, she reached up to touch her lips to his.

For a moment he didn't react at all. Knowing she might be rejected, Hope still followed her heart and, placing her hands on his shoulder, kissed him harder until he finally responded, gathering her into his arms while his mouth opened on hers.

They both forgot what had gone before. If her lip hurt, Hope didn't notice. Her heart was hammering too hard, her head swimming, her body shaking. She wanted him to kiss her, harder and harder. She wanted him to touch her, take her, love her, even if it was only for this one time.

She lay down on the bed once more and he followed, his mouth still covering hers. She felt his heart above hers, beating the same rhythm. She longed to touch him. She tried to unbutton his shirt, but her fingers were shaking too much. He broke off the kiss and sat astride her, unbuttoning the cuffs before dragging his shirt over his head. It ripped in the process, but he didn't care, discarding it on the floor.

Bare to the waist, he was a powerfully masculine figure. Broad and well-muscled, his chest was covered in coarse dark hair that tapered down to his waist. Hope's gaze became shaded with desire.

As she raised her head to his, she saw the same desire reflected in his eyes. She wondered that she'd ever thought them cold. Dark as a storm-cloud, they made her tremble as they trailed from her face to her body, half exposed by her dishevelled clothing, then returned to catch and hold hers, as he began to undress her. He did it gently, his hands barely brushing her skin as they pulled aside her dressing-gown and undid the row of buttons on her night-shirt.

She wore plain striped cotton, but it didn't matter. He didn't notice; his eyes still held hers. He waited until all the buttons were undone before parting the sides of her clothing, then he finally looked at her. With a flat stomach and narrow hips, she had the figure of a boy but for her breasts. Beautifully rounded and full, with large aureoles, a dark pink against her white skin, they gave her body a striking sensuousness.

Guy didn't hide his attraction to her. Grey eyes caressed her body before he even touched her. Then his gaze shifted back to her face as he placed a hand on her waist and slowly travelled upwards over her ribcage to her breasts. He watched the excitement parting her lips, the sheen of sweat on her brow, as his palm spread against her soft skin. He felt the shifting of her hips beneath his as she waited for the moment. Then he smiled with satisfaction at the gasp when his fingers finally stroked the hard nub of her breast.

Though they'd been lovers for so short a time, he knew and remembered what gave her pleasure. When she shut her eyes and moaned a little, he bowed his head to give her more.

Hope cried aloud when his mouth first covered her nipple and bit into her erect flesh. She put her wrist against her own mouth but it didn't stop the sounds of her rising excitement as he continued to play and suck on one breast while his hand made hard the other until she offered it to him, aching for his clever mouth. He kissed her breasts until she forgot the years and the bitterness that lay between them, and wanted only this.

She arched her hips to his, and his mouth went back to hers as his hand left her breast and smoothed the curve of her waist to slide over her hips. He held her against him and she felt another kick of desire at his hard body, ready to enter hers. But he controlled his own urges, and, pushing her back on the bed, began a slow trail with his lips down her skin until he touched the most intimate part of her and gave her such pleasure that her body shuddered with it.

Her breath was coming in gasps when he left her once more to strip off the rest of his clothing. He held her eyes until he returned, straddling her body and drawing his hands down her sweat-dampened skin before he finally lifted her hips to his. Her eyes glazed, her lips parted, she didn't hide her need of him as he poised above her.

'Say you want me.' It was the only time he spoke.

'I want you,' was the only time she spoke.

Then he entered her in a hard thrust that was pain as well as pleasure as he reached into the core of her, as no man had done in over a decade. But she masked the pain, forgotten as he began to move inside her. She lay for a moment, overwhelmed by the unfamiliar sensation, then she started to move with him, rose to meet him, fell with him, in a dance as old as time.

Over and over they joined, bodies slick with sweat, arms and legs entangled, mouths gasping for breath. Over and over, until they became one entity, lost in each other, finally complete. Over and over, until it became unbearable, their bodies on fire, out of control, locked together as they fell into sweet oblivion.

Hope did not regret it. Even when her heart slowed and sanity returned, she did not want to escape. She had spent thirteen years telling herself she hated this man, because if she hadn't, if she'd made herself really look at her feelings, she would have known she had never stopped loving him. If this was to be one night, his chance to cut free of her, then so be it. Having cheated him out of a daughter, she wasn't sure she deserved better.

He turned to look at her, and Hope half expected recriminations, but he said nothing. His eyes asked questions, but he never voiced them. He knew, as she did, that if they talked it would all go wrong again.

He gathered her in his arms, his head above hers as she lay on his chest, listening to the slowing rhythm of his heart. She didn't imagine she would sleep, but he stroked her hair, until somehow she did drift off.

She half woke in the night, making some sound in her sleep that woke him. They made love again, sleepily at first, then with renewed urgency. If anything, it was more satisfying than the first time. Afterwards they still didn't speak but fell asleep, exhausted, lying on their sides with her body curved to his.

The next time Hope woke it was dawn, and his side of the bed was empty. Her heart sank, thinking he'd abandoned her, then she saw him sitting on the window-seat, looking out to sea. He was dressed in trousers, but was still bare-chested and shoeless.

For a moment Hope was tempted to be a coward. She could shut her eyes and pretend to be asleep and let him leave her without explanations.

Instead she reached for her towelling robe and quietly put it on. He didn't notice she was awake until she'd slipped out of bed. He turned as she approached and she saw on his face a bleak look of recrimination. He turned back to the window and she felt her whole world come apart.

'Thirteen years wasted.' He spoke the words to the sea below rather than to her.

She assumed he meant between him and Maxine. The guilt was still crippling. 'You're never going to forgive me, are you?' she said as she came to stand at his side.

'Forgive you?' His eyes turned on her, more distracted than angry. 'Forgive you what?'

'For not telling you about Maxine,' she said in shamed tones.

He held her gaze for a moment, then said quietly, 'Don't you know, Hope Delacroix? I'd forgive you anything.'

He reached a hand out and drew her down to sit beside him, but Hope was too frightened to believe what his eyes were telling her.

'I didn't realise...' She needed him to understand. 'Jack didn't want a baby. Not the first one or Maxine. I thought...'

'That I'd be the same.' His expression hardened for an instant, then he shook his head. 'Do we have to talk about this? I'd prefer we didn't.'

Because they'd end up fighting, he meant, and Hope realised that might well be the case. But it had to be said. She didn't want to spend a few hours or days or whatever he planned immobilised by this time bomb between them. She wanted it exploded, even if she was injured in the fall-out.

'No. I never thought you were the same,' she replied soberly. 'I had no idea how you'd react. Jack assumed it was his and wanted me to get rid of it. I couldn't face telling you. I thought you'd conclude it was Jack's, too.'

'Were you so certain whose the baby was?' he asked.

She nodded. 'It could only have been yours,' she said, and, at his doubtful look, stated forcefully, 'I wasn't pregnant when we became lovers.'

He still looked ready to question the circumstances and, temper rising, Hope pulled her hand away from his. 'Look, if you don't believe me——'

'It's not that,' he said quickly, when she was on the point of rising from the window-seat. 'I don't understand... You went back to Jack——'

'No, I didn't,' she cut across him. 'I let him drive me to London and stayed in a flat he rented, but we were never together again. Not in that sense. And it wasn't the pregnancy. I knew before we drove away from Heron's View that I could never live with Jack again...'

'Because he'd been unfaithful to you?'

'No, because I didn't love him any more.'

Her eyes told him whom she had loved, then and now, but he seemed willfully blind to the fact.

'And you didn't love me,' he concluded, 'otherwise you would have stayed.'

'How could I have?' She rounded on him angrily. 'You didn't want me. That was plain. You couldn't wait to hand me back to Jack.'

'That's not the way it was——' he matched her anger '—and you know it. I stood on that drive down there and waited for you to tell him that it was me you wanted, not him. You didn't say a damn word!'

'And I was waiting for you,' she retaliated, 'but your silence was so deafening, I assumed you'd decided I wasn't worth it.'

'Worth it?' He sprang up from the window-seat and took a pace back from her before exploding, 'I loved you, Hope Delacroix. I loved you so much it was all I could do to hide my feelings from you and my sod of a brother. I came back to get you, not caring if it cost me my home or family, and there you were, about to get into the car with Jack. What was I meant to do? Drop to my knees and beg? Humiliate myself so you could both have a good laugh?'

Hope saw the whole sorry mess of it and it was too much to bear—that they had missed out on the chance of happiness through pride and misunderstanding. It made her furious, with him, with herself, with love itself.

'I came after you!' She shouted the words back at him. '*I* did the begging. OK, not in words, but you had to be blind not to see that I loved you. Only you were too busy playing the wounded hero, weren't you? Do you remember the last words you said to me?' she threw at him.

'Yes,' he answered, but she ignored him.

'You said, "Don't come back,"' she quoted, her voice an echo of the pain she'd felt at the time. 'And you wonder why I didn't come to tell you about Maxine? You wonder why I kept her secret?' She appealed for him to see how it had been for her.

Guy did all right. He shut his eyes for a moment, as he finally realised what had really happened between them.

'What fools we were.' He was no longer angry with her, but with fate, pride, or whatever it was that had driven them apart.

'Yes,' Hope agreed sadly, without any expectations that sorting out the past could lead to a future for them. It was still Elizabeth Downing he intended to marry.

She stared at him blankly when he said, 'So, let's get it right this time.'

'This time?' she repeated, frightened to hope, even when he took her hand and pulled her to her feet.

'You and me.' He made his meaning plainer as he cupped her cheek with his hand and gazed at her with what looked so very much like love.

But Hope was still too scared to believe in happy endings. 'Elizabeth . . . you're marrying Elizabeth.'

'Who says?'

'You did.'

'Not exactly,' he denied, pulling a slight face. 'You concluded, I remained silent.'

'But . . .' Hope tried to catch up with the conversation.

'I have no plans to marry Elizabeth Downing,' he made it quite plain to her. 'I never have. I went out with her a few times and I quite liked her, but when you came back into my life I realised what I'd always suspected. There was only going to be one woman for me, no matter how badly she treated me or how much she hurt me.'

'I hurt you?' Hope retorted in disbelief.

'All right,' he conceded, 'we hurt each other. Because we're both proud, stupid fools. But let's stop now.'

Stop? Hope's eyes clouded for a moment, then he ran on, 'Let's just accept it. I love you and, unless I'm very much mistaken, you love me.'

He loved her. The words echoed in Hope's head, turned over her heart.

'Well?' Guy prompted when she failed to say anything.

'Of course I love you!' Hope answered in a soft, serious voice.

'Thank God for that.' He laughed aloud, and, pulling her close, kissed her long and hard on the mouth.

'There's been no one else,' she confided as he left her almost breathless. 'No lovers. No real boyfriends. You mightn't believe me, after what Jack said——'

He placed his fingers to her lips. 'I believe you... If Jack suggested otherwise, it was to keep us apart... He must have known about Maxine by then.' Guy's brow creased as he tried to make sense of the past.

'Which makes his later behaviour even more inexplicable.'

'What do you mean?' Hope wanted no secrets between them.

'I'm not sure exactly.' Guy shook his head at his own thoughts, before saying, 'If he wanted to keep us apart, why make a will that brings us together? Yet he did, just days before his death... So was it out of devilment or decency?'

'I don't understand.' Hope frowned. 'You speak as if Jack knew he was going to die.'

Guy hesitated, before admitting simply, 'He did.'

'But how...?'

'Last spring Jack was told he had inoperable cancer. He wrote his will shortly afterwards, then the codicil just days before his death... Maybe the car accident was a lucky coincidence. I doubt Amanda would have been much good at nursing a dying man.'

'Poor Jack.' The words slipped out before Hope could catch them.

Fortunately he took them the right way. 'Yes, I suppose he was. He certainly threw away everything worthwhile in his life.' His grey eyes rested on Hope's face, the love in them total. 'I won't make the same mistake... When we marry, it'll be for keeps,' he added quietly.

'I—I... You mean... you want to...' Hope hadn't expected a proposal.

'Of course,' he confirmed, his old arrogant self again. 'I'd say it was the logical conclusion.'

'*You* would.' She laughed at his less than romantic approach, but loved him for it too. She had been married to someone who was all charm and no substance. That was how she knew the real thing, and she was looking at it now. A man so strong and straight and sensitive that he could be everything to a woman—support, friend, lover.

'So, let's not start with any taboos,' he continued briskly. 'You were married to my brother, however briefly. I can live with the fact, so let's not spend the next fifty years finding ways not to mention it. If I wanted you, it was despite your being married to him, not because of it. Ok?'

'OK,' Hope nodded, and, chastened, murmured, 'I'm a fool, I know.'

She had been a fool to believe Jack, a fool to imagine someone as confident and forceful as Guy would be in his brother's shadow. If anything, Jack had envied Guy his strength, his imperviousness to criticism or approval. Jack had been the insecure one, his ego needing constant bolstering by a succession of young women.

'Truthfully, I was less than overjoyed to fall in love with my brother's wife,' Guy said bluntly, 'but we have to accept the inevitability of it. We belong together.'

He made it sound as serious as a life sentence. Hope matched his tone, sighing heavily. 'I suppose so,' she agreed, then smiled to herself as she said, 'The trouble is we're going to have to work hard to make up for lost time.'

'Work hard?' It took him a moment to understand, then he caught her amused glance towards the bed.

\* \* \*

They missed two flights before they actually boarded a plane for Malta. Hope was alternately elated and terrified. With every look and touch, she knew that the man she loved loved her, but there was still a final hurdle to jump. Maxine.

Being a coward, Hope would have deferred telling her the whole truth, but Guy overruled her. She didn't blame him. After missing thirteen years of his daughter's life, he wanted to claim her as soon as possible. The trouble was that Hope saw herself losing that daughter at the very same time.

'Stop worrying,' Guy instructed as an airport taxi finally set them down at the Port of Valletta. 'I'll handle it.'

He smiled and squeezed her hand in reassurance. Hope managed a smile back, but she didn't stop worrying.

Maxine was on deck with Natalie when they eventually located their hired boat, the *Gibraltar Rose*. Hope gave her a nervous smile, anxious to make up for their quarrel on the telephone, and Maxine didn't need any more encouragement. She jumped down from the boat and went into Hope's arms.

'Let's not fight again, Mum,' she pleaded, a catch in her voice. 'I hate it when we're not friends. I'm sorry about going on about Greenbrooke's. If we have to return to London, that's OK by me.'

'Oh, Maxine.' Hope hugged her daughter hard and felt such love for her that it just increased her fear. 'I was being selfish. You can go to Greenbrooke's, if that's what you want.'

Maxine's face lit up, then sobered again, 'But what about you? If you're going back to London——'

'She isn't,' Guy cut in. 'Your mother's agreed to stay at Heron's View. In fact, she's agreed to marry me.'

Maxine looked from one to another, and her jaw dropped open. 'You and Mum... You're...' She couldn't find an appropriate word.

'In love,' Guy supplied, a lazy smile on his face. Maxine looked delighted for a moment, before her gaze switched back to a more subdued Hope.

'Mum?' Maxine questioned the doubts on Hope's face. 'Is this true?'

Hope nodded soberly, adding, 'If it's OK with you?'

'OK?' Maxine echoed. 'It's ab fab!' she declared in delight, and ran off to tell the world.

Smiling broadly, Guy arched a brow at Hope. It said, I told you so. He had accurately predicted Maxine's reaction to their marrying.

Hope made a slight face in return. They had only jumped the first hurdle.

Before they could jump another, Maxine had broadcast the news to the Castillons and they were being warmly congratulated by all concerned. No one seemed surprised, just delighted.

Guy waited until they'd drunk a hastily chilled glass of champagne, then, catching Hope's fretful expression, got on with the business in hand.

Hope told herself she was spineless as she watched him take Maxine ashore under the guise of buying her mother flowers. She feared everybody's celebratory mood was going to be very short-lived.

Beth, realising something was up, got rid of Natalie and Richard and sat with her.

'I assume you've told Guy the truth,' Beth prompted, at her less than joyous expression. 'Is he going to tell Maxine?'

'The truth?' Hope looked at her uncertainly.

'Maxine being Guy's,' Beth stated without preamble. 'She is, isn't she?'

'I...' Hope thought of lying for a second, then realised it was pointless. 'Yes. How did you know?'

'Obvious, my dear Watson.' Beth's smile was warm. 'The chances of an uncle and niece being that alike— looks, manner, the lot—must be remote. Plus, though

Guy clearly hadn't realised, his love for you kept coming out in his treatment of her.'

'Oh.' Hope didn't know what to say. It seemed that only she and Guy had been that blind. 'Are you shocked?'

'Hardly.' Beth laughed at the idea. 'In fact, I'm pleased for you both. If I may say so, Jack Delacroix was a heel of the first order. You deserved better, and you've finally got it... Just hold on to it this time, girl,' Beth advised with a kindly smile.

'I'll try,' Hope agreed, but her mind was still with Guy and Maxine. Loving Guy didn't suddenly make everything right. If Maxine turned against her, she couldn't bear it.

They came back two hours later. Hope was on her own, Beth having followed her husband and daughter ashore. Guy had his arm round Maxine's shoulders, but she wasn't smiling. Hope felt her happiness slipping from her as Guy disappeared below deck and Maxine came to stand in front of her.

'Guy explained everything,' Maxine relayed in a tight voice. 'You should have told me, Mum...told me years ago.'

'Yes, I know.' Hope had no excuses.

But it seemed as if Guy had made excuses for her, as Maxine ran on, 'G—Dad says it wasn't really your fault. That he and his brother treated you badly.'

Hope could have left it like that, but she shook her head. 'No, Guy never treated me badly. I just didn't— didn't have the courage to trust in him. I was very young and very silly.'

'Did you love him?' Maxine asked the most important question of all.

'Yes.' Hope could answer it with absolute honesty.

It was enough for Maxine, her resentment fading even as she repeated, 'You should have told us—me and Dad.'

'I know.' Hope still didn't dispute it.

'But I suppose it was difficult, like Dad says,' Maxine mused in reply, then gave a mouth-droppingly casual shrug, before announcing, 'Well, there's no point in worrying about it now... Can we go ashore for dinner?'

'I... Yes.' Hope blinked at the rapid change of subject.

'Great, I'll go and get changed,' Maxine announced, before ducking below deck.

Guy appeared moments later. Hope looked as disconcerted as she felt.

'She seems to have forgiven me,' she said in wonder.

'Yes, I heard.' Guy admitted to eavesdropping. 'That's the great thing about kids. They live strictly in the present.'

'Yes.' Hope wondered if they, as adults, could escape the past.

Guy was clearly thinking along the same lines, as he suggested quietly, 'Why don't we follow her example and forgive each other?'

'Can we?' Hope knew she could forgive him; most of his sins had been in her own imagination. But could he forgive her?

'Of course we can.' He reached down to pull her to her feet. 'We've lost a decade or so, but in fifty years it'll just be a brief interlude in our lives.'

'An interlude...' Hope echoed his words and, holding his gaze, saw what he saw: a whole lifetime together, living and loving, fighting and making up, growing old, passion fading, but love remaining. Never-ending love.

And wasn't it wonderful? They were just on day one of the rest of their lives.

# HARLEQUIN PRESENTS®

## PENNY JORDAN

"Penny Jordan pens a formidable read."
—*Romantic Times*

Harlequin brings you the best books by the best authors!

### Watch for:
## #1839 THE TRUSTING GAME

Christa had learned the hard way that men were not to be trusted. So why should she believe Daniel when he said he could teach her to trust?

Harlequin Presents—the best has just gotten better!
Available in October wherever
Harlequin books are sold.

Look us up on-line at: http://www.romance.net

TAUTH-13

# Take 4 bestselling love stories FREE
## Plus get a FREE surprise gift!

# REBECCA

## 43 LIGHT STREET

# YORK

## FACE TO FACE

*Bestselling author Rebecca York returns to "43 Light Street"*
*for an original story of past secrets, deadly deceptions—and*
*the most intimate betrayal.*

She woke in a hospital—with amnesia…and with child.
According to her rescuer, whose striking face is the last
image she remembers, she's Justine Hollingsworth. But
nothing about her life seems to fit, except for the baby
inside her and Mike Lancer's arms around her. Consumed
by forbidden passion and racked by nameless fear, she
must discover if she is Justine…or the victim of some mind
game. Her life—and her unborn child's—depends on it….

Don't miss *Face To Face*—Available in October, wherever
Harlequin books are sold.

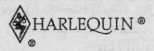

## HARLEQUIN ®
®

Look us up on-line at: http://www.romance.net

# Free Gift Offer

With a Free Gift proof-of-purchase
from any Harlequin® book, you can receive
a beautiful cubic zirconia pendant.

This stunning marquise-shaped stone is a genuine cubic
zirconia—accented by an 18" gold tone necklace.
(Approximate retail value $19.95)

## Send for yours today...
## compliments of ✦HARLEQUIN®

To receive your free gift, a cubic zirconia pendant, send us one original proof-of-purchase, photocopies not accepted, from the back of any Harlequin Romance®, Harlequin Presents®, Harlequin Temptation®, Harlequin Superromance®, Harlequin Intrigue®, Harlequin American Romance®, or Harlequin Historicals® title available in August, September or October at your favorite retail outlet, together with the Free Gift Certificate, plus a check or money order for $1.65 U.S./$2.15 CAN. (do not send cash) to cover postage and handling, payable to Harlequin Free Gift Offer. We will send you the specified gift. Allow 6 to 8 weeks for delivery. Offer good until October 31, 1996 or while quantities last. Offer valid in the U.S. and Canada only.

# Free Gift Certificate

Name: _____

Address: _____

City: _____ State/Province: _____ Zip/Postal Code: _____

Mail this certificate, one proof-of-purchase and a check or money order for postage and handling to: HARLEQUIN FREE GIFT OFFER 1996. In the U.S.: 3010 Walden Avenue, P.O. Box 9071, Buffalo NY 14269-9057. In Canada: P.O. Box 604, Fort Erie, Ontario L2Z 5X3.

---

**FREE GIFT OFFER**                                    084-KMF

ONE PROOF-OF-PURCHASE

To collect your fabulous FREE GIFT, a cubic zirconia pendant, you must include this
original proof-of-purchase for each gift with the properly completed Free Gift Certificate.

---

084-KMF

**Sabrina        It Happened One Night
Working Girl        Pretty Woman
While You Were Sleeping**

If you adore romantic comedies then have
we got the books for you!

Look for Harlequin's
**LOVE & LAUGHTER™**
at your favorite retail outlet. It's a brand-new
series with two books every month capturing
the lighter side of love.

You'll enjoy humorous love stories by favorite
authors and brand-new writers, including
JoAnn Ross, Lori Copeland, Jennifer Crusie,
Kasey Michaels and many more!

**LOVE & LAUGHTER™**—a natural
combination...always
romantic...always entertaining

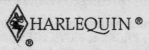

HARLEQUIN ®

LL-1

# You're About to Become a *Privileged Woman*

Reap the rewards of fabulous free gifts and benefits with proofs-of-purchase from Harlequin and Silhouette books

## Pages & Privileges™

It's our way of thanking you for buying our books at your favorite retail stores.

**Harlequin and Silhouette—
the most privileged readers in the world!**

For more information about Harlequin and Silhouette's PAGES & PRIVILEGES program call the Pages & Privileges Benefits Desk: 1-503-794-2499

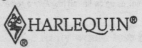

HARLEQUIN®

HP-PP179